BOOK OF DREAMS

Jack Kerouac

Library of Congress Catalog Card Number: 60-14774
ISBN: 0-87286-027-2

Cover photo of Jack Kerouac by Robert Frank

CITY LIGHTS BOOKS are published at the City Lights Bookstore, 261 Columbus Avenue, San Francisco, California, 94133.

FOREWORD

The reader should know that this is just a collection of dreams that I scribbled after I woke up from my sleep—They were all written spontaneously, nonstop, just like dreams happen, sometimes written before I was even wide awake—The characters that I've written about in my novels reappear in these dreams in weird new dream situations (check the Table of Characters on the next page) and they continue the same story which is the one story that I always write about. The heroes of "On the Road," "The Subterraneans," etc. reappear here doing further strange things for no other particular reason than that the mind goes on, the brain ripples, the moon sinks, and everybody hides their heads under pillows with sleepingcaps.

Good.

And good because the fact that everybody in the world dreams every night ties all mankind together shall we say in one unspoken Union and also proves that the world is really transcendental which the Communists do not believe because they think their dreams are "unrealities" instead of visions of what they saw in their sleep.

So I dedicate this book of dreams to the roses of the unborn.

TABLE OF CHARACTERS

NAME IN "BOOK OF DREAMS"	NAME IN "ON THE ROAD"
Cody Pomeray	Dean Moriarty
Irwin Garden	Carlo Marx
Jack (Kerouac) (me)	Sal Paradise
Bull Hubbard	Old Bull Lee
Ed Buckle	Ed Dunkel
Joanna	Marylou
Huck	Elmo Hassel
Deni Bleu	Remi Boncoeur
Ma	Sal Paradise's "aunt"
Irwin Swenson	Rollo Greb
Julien Love	Damion
Evelyn Pomeray	Camille Moriarty
Guy Green	Tim Grey
Irving Minko	Roland Major

NAME IN "BOOK OF DREAMS"	NAME IN "THE SUBTERRANEANS"
Irene May	Mardou Fox
Jack (Kerouac)	Leo Percepied
Raphael Urso	Yuri Gligoric
Irwin Garden	Adam Moorad
Julien Love	Sam Vedder
Bull Hubbard	Frank Carmody
Irwin Swenson	Austin Bromberg
James Watson	Balliol MacJones
Shelley Lisle	Ross Wallenstein
Gerard Rose	Julien Alexander
Dick Beck	Fritz Nicholas
Danny Richman	Larry O'Hara
Ronald Macy	Charles Bernard

NAME IN "BOOK OF DREAMS"	NAME IN "THE DHARMA BUMS"
Irwin Garden	Alvah Goldbook
Simon Darlovsky	George
Jack (Kerouac)	Ray Smith
Rosemarie	Rosie Buchanan

OH! THE HORRIBLE VOYAGES I've had to take across the country and back with gloomy railroads and stations you never dreamed of—one of em a horrible pest of bats and crap holes and incomprehensible parks and rains, I can't see the end of it on all horizons, this is the book of dreams.

Jesus life is dreary, how can a man live let alone work—sleeps and dreams himself to the other side —and that's where your Wolf is ten times worse than preetypop knows—and how, look, I stopped—how can a man lie and say shit when he has gold in his mouth. Cincinnati, Philarkadelphia, Frohio, stations in the Flue—rain town, graw flub, Beelzabur and Hemptown I've been to all of them and read Finnegain's Works what will it do me good if I dont stop and righten the round wrong in my poor bedighted b—what word is it?—skull...

Talk, talk, talk—

I went and saw Cody and Evelyn, it all began in Mexico, on Bull's ratty old couch I purely dreamed that I was riding a white horse down a side street in that North town like in Maine but really off Highway Maine with the rainy night porches in the up and down America, you've all seen it you ignorant pricks that cant understand what you're reading, there, with sidestreets, trees, night, mist, lamps, cowboys, barns, hoops, girls, leaves, something so familiar and never been seen it tears your heart out—I'm dashing down this street, cloppity clip, just left Cody and Evelyn at a San Francisco spectral restaurant or cafeteria table at Market and Third where we talked eagerly plans for a trip East it was (as if!) (as if there could be East or West in that waving old compass of the sack, base set on the pillow, foolish people and crazy people dream, the world wont be saved at this rate, these are the scravenings of a—lost—sheep)—the Evelyn of these dreams is an amenable—Cody is—(cold and jealous)—something—dont know—dont care—Just that after I talk to them—Good God it's taken me all this time to say, I'm riding down the hill—it becomes the Bunker Hill Street of Lowell—I'm headed for the black river on a white horse—it broke my heart when I woke up, to realize that I was going to make that trip East (pathetic!)—by myself—alone in eternity—to which now I go, 'on white horse, not knowing what's going to happen, predestined or not, if predestined why bother, if not why try, not if try why, but try if why not, or not why —At the present time I have nothing to say and refuse to go on without further knowledge.

AND MEXICO CITY, A SPECTRAL ONE WITH WISHED FOR PIERS sitting at the base of gloomy gray Liverpool-like Ferrocarril—I and a horde of young generation in suits with prom flower girls attend a melee, a gathering, at a building, a tower—so crowded, I, among bachelors, have to wait outside—rousing applause, speeches, music inside—Strange how in my dreams it doesnt seem that everything's already happened in a more interesting way, but awe, sweet awe remains—for my rage is eating my heart away, What am I doing in this sinister North Carolina as a clerk getting up at 6:00—a clerk among sinister oldfaced clerks in an old gloomy railroad office—no dream could be as frightening and more like hell. —I finally manage to get in the party—no, the idiot dog woke me up at just the point where I might have made a story of the deal—and lately anyway I wake at dawn with the horrors. In New York they're stealing my ideas, getting published, being feted, fucking other men's wives, getting laurel wreaths from old poets—and I wake on this bed of horror to a nightmare only life could have devised. To Hell with it.

IN A STRANGE LIVINGROOM presumably in Mexico City but very much and suspiciously like a livingroom in a dream of my Ma and Pa in Lowell or Dream Movetown—June (Evans) is telling me the name of a great unknown Greek writer, Plipias, Snipias, how his father ran away with the family money so Plipias, queer, went to live on an Island with the boy he loves; and wrote: "I never go on strike against man, because I love him"—June recommended this writer highly, and said: "You can spend an hour a day hassling over small things but in the larger sense you can see what he means, never go on strike against man—" Meanwhile I'm about to go in the bathroom but Bull's already in there—has made no comment—

DIGGING IN THIS WOMAN'S CELLAR to plant, or transplant, my marijuana—under clutters of papers (just a minute before was going thru my own things, in a huge new room)—clutters of rubber bands, etc., and digging into dirt to make plant bed but realized how deep her hole was beneath her junk, thought to myself, "The old lady's—the older you get the deeper your cellar gets, more like a grave———the more your cellar looks like a grave—" There was a definite hole to the left—a definite saying—

I was foraging for my stories and paper—earlier I was in a room, working for a man as secretary, he was a masquerader, a fraud—and an evil pulp magazine crook genius leader of some evil—My mother visited me as if I was in jail—I turned over in my bed, my cot, interested in these things—

HORRIBLE HASSELS IN CHICAGO—with young seamen and Deni Bleu, in a car, Boston-like going up and down bright traffics—stopped by cops, the youngest kid throws 2 quarts beer out window and smashes them—"Goddam him!" we all curse—I make note of my pockets, nothing but a rubber-But cops find a roach, but I'm going to say it's just thyme, or Cu-Babs, and that's what it really is—thyme not valuable but culpable—a plainclothes taxidriver cop has me me stick my tongue out to check on Cu-Babs, I do so, he makes as if to slap me but doesnt—On the radio we'd heard big seaman union broadcasts with that silly wiper from the S. S. Roamer giggling over the air—also making angry union speeches—Deni gloomy as ever—used as ever—

Then in the olddream Frisco of hills again but still related to the Bunker Hill of the white horse and altho it hasnt happened since I actually went back to Frisco—Cody is driving jaloppy, a swank apartment house hill (he pulls throttle from floor without seeming effort to reach)—he's telling me something but unpleasantly, everything is now unpleasant, everybody wants money or earning power from me, the sweetness is gone—Cody has a harried, unpleasant, sullen expression— The jaloppy reminds me of the jaloppy I had parked in a quiet Ozone Park street last week, a buddy sleeping at the wheel, and a guy began shooting at us with a shotgun from 2nd story window of a leafy Calabrese home and I ducked in gutter gritting my teeth for feel of shot burning me but he missed—then I run down street, he begins shooting at me deliberately (first shot was aimed at woman June Ogilvie woman on sidewalk)—now he wants me—I run—I'm tearful and terrified that he's after me—Jaloppy is mine—he jumps in, "he's going to steal my truck now!" I moan —"Goddam this world!" And my buddy didnt move from behind that wheel—was this because he was killed by the first shot? He was Don Jackson of Mex City—I wished I hadnt left carkeys in car—I'd been driving and driving, thru that spectral railroad station Rainycity—The madman shot again—I was in that Ozone Park that sometimes at night on a vast boulevard I'm riding a bus to my mother's davenport porch house—all rattling, all haunted by the dead—lost lost lost in the infinite eternity of our doom—

LAST NIGHT MY FATHER WAS BACK in Lowell—O Lord, O haunted life—and he wasnt interested in anything much—He keeps coming back in this dream, to Lowell, has no shop, no job even—a few ghostly friends are rumored to be helping him, looking for connections, he has many especially among the quiet misanthropic old men—but he's feeble and he aint supposed to live long anyway so it doesnt matter—He has departed from the living so much his once-excitement, tears, argufying, it's all gone, just paleness, he doesnt care any more—has a lost and distant air—We saw him in a cafeteria, across street from Paige's but not Waldorf's—he hardly talks to me—it's mostly my mother talking to me about him—"Ah well, ah bien, he vivra pas longtemps ce foi _icit!_"—"he wont live long _this_ time!"—she hasnt changed—tho she too mourns to see his change—but God Oh God this haunted life I keep hoping against hope against hope he's gong to live anyway even tho I not only know he's sick but that it's a dream and he did die in real life—ANYWAY—I worry myself... (When writing _Town and the City_ I wanted to say "Peter worried himself white"—for the haunted sadness that I feel in these dreams is white—) Maybe Pop is very quietly sitting in a chir while we talk—he happened to come home from downtown to sit awhile but not because it's home so much as he has no other place to go at the moment—in fact he hangs out in the poolhall all day—reads the paper a little—he himself doesnt want to live much longer—that's the point—He's so different than he was in real life—in haunted life I think I see now his true soul—which is like mine—life means nothing to him—or, I'm my father myself and this is me (especially the Frisco dreams)—but it is Pa, the big fat man, but frail and pale, but so mysterious and un-Kerouac—but is that me? Haunted life, haunted life—and all this takes place within inches of the ironclouds dream of 1946 that saved my soul (the bridge across the Y, 10 blocks up from 'cafeteria'—) Oh Dammit God—

THEY WOULDNT LET ME WORK on the ship even tho it had just sailed from the North River pier where Joe and I've many times walked—a gray, dismal pier—rickety, hive-ish, with "Julien's reformatory" as I call a certain strange Arabic tenement and the place where Ma and I stood on the warship deck in that famous dream of face-towel crabs floating in the water that Hubbard analyzed in 1945 —I'm in my quarters, we're already at sea, I feel lonely, awful, lost in mazes of fresh-paint rooms and lockers and bunks and worried about the gray cold sea and the officials come in to check my papers and he, the head one, young, grins—I call him Mate, meaning First Mate, forgetting the Sir—"You cant sail without a so-and-so paper," he says with incredulous smile, "You'll have to sail this trip but you cant work"—I'd helped with lines at tight dock —in fact I'd run on board the very last minute as the ship was moving down the crowded canal, I could see its funnel passing roofs—how I got on is unclear, I was returning from a spectral ball in the huge-room places like the Mexico Harbour City Tower with mixups of everybody—O haunted poorboy John Kerouac but you are headed for a long sad dream—

The smoke is on the Tar River, the sparrow does its delicate flutter—

THEN I'M WORKING ON THE RAILROAD, as I've been doing now I realize for years in dreams of the Barrostook Crock & Crane R.R. that runs sidewise east and west from Lowell to Lynn pot and other such places along a dry almost Mexican SP desert ground with tragic brakeman shacks, the road to some All Boston—now I'm almost California SP and Cody and my father mingled into the One Father image of Accusation is mad at me because I missed my local, my freight, I fucked up with the Mother Image down the line, I did something childish (the little boy writing in the room) and held up iron railroads of men—I finally get to the track but the freight is rolling so fast by that time I'm afraid to try jumping on—grimy Pop-Cody is already at work, he may fuck up in his own tragic night but by Jesus Christ when it's time to go to work it's fucking time to go to work— There are also angry faces of seamen on ships, I screwed up at the potato pump—W C Fields in switchman's overalls by the tracks, the doll-like brakemen are jumping on the fast train,—I'm left gooping in my own sor-row—groping in my own dull Tit—

A LONG ALL-NIGHT AFFAIR WITH A WOMAN supposed to be Marlene Dietrich— "because of her mouth you can tell"—but other people seem skeptical she's Marlene, though I believe it or insist on believing it—I go to some parking lot and tell the owner of the used cars that Marlene's my girl— it's located on Bridge St. Lowell across the street from the big gray warehouse— There, I am shown a Life magazine with a big 3-page spread of pictures of me in a raincoat (tan, tailored) cutting along like a "lonely writer in sadness" in various angle shots—dark-haired, gloomy, line faced—I'm displeased because I'd have preferred closeups and also because I didnt know these pictures had been taken—by Marlene, presumably—her mouth which was the key to her identity was tragically muggled and almost with buck teeth, like Bill Wagstrom's mouth in Mexico City or the mouth of the used car man in Rocky Mount (he was a big tall man with Panama hat) (and's in dream) and Shorty's wife in Easonburg, and Nina Foch's mouth somehow tho she's not muggled but like real life Marlene.

AN ENCAMPMENT OF ALMOST PROVINCETOWN SUBTERRANEANS (Monterrey hipsters) around a fire, Peaches, etc., I'm with them but getting up to hit the road (the night traffic) for Canada, back to Canada and early pale Twenties furniture (sad beads of afternoon) scenes of my childhood where my mother is—it's a long trip, a sad trip, I start but come back to say something, they dont care, there's a cat in the road, I've had a dab of Immortality in this dream—This is opening chapter of real "On the Road"—

A LONG VOYAGE to Mexico City, I leave my California railroad work before it's even started (like I did the Carolina r.r. work) and en route get involved in houses and small dirt streets like you dont see any more because they made the automobile to ride 5 miles down the broad dead road with for what they used to slink across the street for)—I make goofy tape records with Eisenhower, he condescends, but is actually friendly and has fun and doesnt mind leaving his goof words to posterity unlike real life politician-arrive in Mexico City, with Guy Green, go to Hubbard's house and plug up my new longplaying phonograph and play the tape for Guy—he is Eisenhower himself—he appreciates and digs and laughs—but the door bursts open and in staggers Hubbard roaring drunk, he—I say to him, to "apologize" for breaking into his house uninvited, "I got this new phonograph and lots of money"

—as if, aren't you grateful I am here?—but he staggers around, makes only cutting comments, spits on the floor, goes to his room, every time Guy (who's heard so much about his greatness from me) tries to talk to him Bull is absolutely stone silent as tho deliberately— affronting Guy terribly because he has sensed that I prepared Guy for him and he ignores everything and is silent with that half smile —I'm mad, never want anything to do with him either any more, fresh paranoias follow me to every travel terminal, I also feel guilty and foolish and importunate for leaving that railroad work so soon, now I'm fucked, all bridges behind me burned to dreary eternity—Earlier my father had returned, to West St. but was also now a drunkard and didnt answer or give a shit—Intractable as a bad child—and I with my mother is the lost spectralities of a 4th of July Grool stand in criticism of him, fireworks on First St., nameless events waving in the road towards Joe's on Bunker Hill and down to Centralville center—the rose lattices on the porch, the drear light of the house like the light in the Cody-copwoman-oval track-children dream of moths—the Mystic Celt is far from bloomed, he's tied a Slavic knot around the Fellaheen band of the world, the Aramaean Springtime is shoving underground the Iron Americas of Fellah—

DREAMED OF BEING IN SOME KIND OF HARDSHIP PILGRIMAGE with a man and woman in some Mongolian harshland and when we got to the (again) Fellaheen town (of the Fellaheen-rippling dream) which had a gray cement factory color and dismalness I said "However in your town here I could pose as a prisoner of yours—in fact, in reality I am your prisoner, according to the facts—"

"Yes, that's a fact," they said much, and innocently, pleased, especially the woman—they might have been Mongolian— I walked on the sidewalk ground carrying my rifle stock down as befitting a prisoner and they rode the point of our vehicular or animal travel-gimmick that had carted us across the wastes—I secretly mistrusted their joy, we had started on some Jesus pilgrimage, now they were letting their thoughts be affected by matters of war—but I trusted them finally—

THEN A WHOLE CREW OF US WERE MOVING FURNITURE in a house but with the same procedure as a crew switching boxcars and riding the brakes, so the tagman boss says to me "Ride that one" and it's a shiny mahogany sofa-table that I push over the smooth hardwood floor into a room on the right (like into Track 2), and it's a bedroom, there are relationships among us like those of children, we're in a sense prisoners, or children, and innocent but have done wrong in the past—The area is wild with possibilities of scenes just recent, the Mexico Circle (Orizaba Park houses around a sweet pond pool at night, window lights) and the blond kid of the 88 (Willie-like) and the new Fellaheen land——

I HAD THE TOLSTOYAN DREAM, a great movie, with the Bolkonsky-Boldieu hero officer, in the stress of events stomping out of a officer's milling ball and giving himself away thereby and they shout like Russians with toasts and arrest him on the spot and he indignant and meaningful—Meanwhile I've been told to note the particular excellence of the performance of the "Peasant"—the old Fellaheen Hero—He is in Cossack soldier uniform, a soldier comes into his strange room to arrest him, the Peasant is just standing there,—with a sense that not only I but my father is watching this film, and it's in the 42nd Apollo and it's like the great lost Lost Father chapter of now-naturally out of print <u>Town and the City</u> and I remember my pre-tea joys, strengths and knowings God bless the purity of the

Martins, the Kerouacs of my soul, still unfulfilled—we are all to watch how the Peasant handles situations, he takes the gun from the soldier's hand, in a funny way, with an enigmatic opaque remark, and points it floorward, makes a face, the soldier is non plussed by this brother peasant,—the audience laughs with anticipatory tears in its eyes, it's the great Tolstoyan Movie.

The peasant has a big head and wears a huge hat & vast sadness in his face just as the officer has vast rage in his—

ON A RAILROAD OR RAIL TRAVEL MACHINE or just flying straight thru the rail of space I see California in the night along the way, a chaingang of very recognizable hoboes and winos like on 3rd street and with ordinary but flushed-with-drinking American faces like Conductor Fields, they're in chains, sadistic fat guards have them completely sick & trembling, I see them being pushed and maltreated just for fun, but only vaguely in the gloom and I distinctly hear a loud cry "You win! You win!" as apparently a guard was torturing a poor devil just to hear some such outcry—I feel sick—just 2 blocks along, where cars are parked on a slant like in the Middlewest wheat towns but in pink neon California Road I see two separate fist fights between tiny children, with adults watching, fighting between the cars—young kids & children, it is the Machine in all its glory—I wake up horrified—nightmares are paranoia—

EVERSOTRAGIC FURTHER DREAM OF THE "INCENSED NOBLE" of the Great Tolstoyan Movie—here I see him in his family life in a house located in the strange truckdriving New Havens or whatevers of old dreams and he's got a family, particularly a beautiful blond child, very Scandinavian, "like the son of the Kansas scientist with blond hair, the land reclaimer"—(one in hitchhike of Aug 1952)—everybody wants to kiss him except me, they're kissing him on his erotic rosy lips, the Noble (somewhat Bull-like) takes peculiar pleasure in waiting for his turn & in kissing kid—he's "queer as the day is long," like Hubbard—in fact right then I see a vision of Bull as developing into a final old goodnatured lecher with no thoughts—just "waiting for his blubbery kiss" from Rainbow Lips—& Bull was in dream much earlier, but somehow in the same house, which has a lot of overstuffed furniture brown, gloomy & to me beautiful—fact, I talk about furniture with somebody, we're sitting, there are other events in other rooms—the whole house spectral & almost a boat again—but definitely located "in Maine"—or at junctures near a tremendous embrillianted Kansas, with sideshows of Fellaheen Gypsies off the main highway, down Mexico like dirt street like near the Rastro at Dave's, the cars flash east & west beneath great whiteradiant skies, Mexico is "south" off that (as in Geography)—the house in on the right, on a knoll, suddenly as we pull up to the house (Aunt Whozoo's inside) me, my father, the Noble, & a driver, a mob of men surround the car to beat us up—open the door, say to me "Get out" —I think of rushing out in a wild fury slugging faces, then I think of my poor pop in the backseat with me, they're going to beat up that poor old sick man?—(when I woke up I pleaded "You cant beat up my father!" "He's got cancer!")—but they dont care, something the Noble has done has grimly set their purposes, they dont care about personalities & fathers, just as I wake up I realize I shall get kicked and beaten & probably killed but somehow the Noble—no, he too will be killed and beaten I guess too—the fool's done something—my father says nothing—Ah what's happening in the world!—that now the men come to beat us up!—what will the horrified women in the window say? Where's the pretty child? the angel? Dreamt in Cameo Hotel.

IMMENSE SAGAS ALL NIGHT LONG, fantastic detailed nightmares of me losing my pants twice in a row & being sought by the police also as a sex pervert because I have so much to do with young high school boys and girls while losing my pants—I talk to them eagerly with some flimsy scarf over my thigh—ugh—a strange exultant queer saint of some kind—The first time I'm getting on a local passenger train, it's going down the line of white radiant land, commuting school kids are jammed in it—I've already been up to something all night—involved with youngsters in the same way as the flophouse of Chicago dreamed in the Greensboro Salvation Army—I get on the train a sort of official brakeman but somehow I lost my pants, I try to cover up but the cloth or scarf keeps slipping to show my thigh, my cock with no hardon, I hope no one sees—it's "just like" the dream in the crummy 5 nights before, Waldo Walters' wife is in a caboose with me, dotty, we talk excitedly and intimately and suddenly just as she's going to show me the important point Waldo comes in and simultaneously her skirt falls open to reveal a tiny cock which is "a woman's" nonetheless I insist—a woman with a cock, that's all—and Waldo sees what we've been up to in a "wrong light," we had "no sexual intentions"—same way, my little cock shows—and I'm blushing to cover up, my milky thighs without hair—somehow I get into the yard of a great lost school like the Horace Mann of my dreams but situated in a radiant New Britain California Land and there still pantless I'm plotting to get them back and some kids see me from the classroom windows (like the windows of the Queens General Hospital which were in an orange wall that bore the imprint dust stain of a former huge portrait there hung, picture of my diploma or brother or mother I forget, or me)—teachers are dissatisfied, call police (all the talk the details, forever elude us!)—I sneak around looking for my pants—Then in a gigantic house with hundred foot ceiling I have all my poems, manuscripts, all of them sexual, crazy, revealing, skewered around among records and books and a whole bunch of high school kids with me laughing at my antics and description of when I lost my pants but now they know I'm crazy and are cruel in jest, the cops are coming, I sneak back down there to recover my culpable revealing manuscripts, "shh" I say to Emil Ladeau, "the lady upstairs'll hear you!"— we look up, in a 4th floor window is poor harmless Mrs. Garden!!!!!!— (Emil Ladeau I insulted once for his nose, in that John MacDougald workshop dream)—Mrs. Garden wont say nothing, I'll have time—"It was horrible, I had no pants here the last time, cops are after me naturally, twice an offender" I'm saying—and a thousand rattly crazy things also——I have the same terror as in an old Henry Street dream where I murdered somebody or was a witness, and hid a revealing manuscript in a trash basket, it was pink, like lobsters, towels and walls of hospitals—Only yesterday I was feeling guilty for writing Doctor Sax, On the Road, a sheepish guilty idiot turning out rejectable unpublishable wildprose madhouse enormities—Ah, come to papa do,—the high school girls were cruel, the boys too—it wasnt my fault I lost my pants, they eluded me on the Aiken St. bridge somehow—it is such a terrifying bridge, you walk on narrow cables, it's immense as the world—At the end, I'm watching from a tenement top window like Julien's Dostoevskyan loft, like the George Jessel New York tenements on the upper east end—all the children are playing on the opposite roof, nets are stretched across the court to catch the ones that fall, when they do the other kids watch smiling—the fallen one cries in the net—I told you it was cruel—the mothers are not too concerned—"why cant they play on the sidewalks," I say,—"there's no room, civilization is too vast now"—Guilt is a dream, pity is the only reality...

A TREMENDOUS FAMILY SAGA, it takes place in a huge high apartment by the sea, the same sea of Tidal Waves and Sea Battles—there are intelligent child girls, earlier in the opening of the Saga, in a big room, after something to do with the Girl of the Huge Room, Halvar Hayes holds a kitten by the neck choking it and me and someone else (Joe Gavota was around) try to break his grip—"You're choking that cat to death!" I cry—and try clawing Hal's face, pushing his nose in, pulling his hair, everything, kicking him in the balls so he'll leave that kitty go and he wont—both of us are pummelling and pulling and torturing at him and he wont let that little dying kitty go—my heart is breaking all over—and Hal has such pitiful guts—I dont understand what, how it ends, there are dispersings and gray scene shiftings in the Shakespearean stage of my dreambrain—and the next day the kitty is still alive and playing! I am astounded, hosannahd, resurrected—and poor Hal was tortured for nothing?—that Judas choking Jesus! or that Jesus being tortured by Judas for a chimerical cat! Then the Saga swings to the high apartment, there are bargain basements below, a veritable Radio City, or Paramount Theater, a Jewish winter resort, crowds,—great company visits us, we have rich furnishings (like Kereskys)—smart little Margaret O'Brien girls—I protect them—we have inheritances—crises come and go—suddenly in the midst of a big cocktail party the depth charges start exploding on the beach ten stories below (this is the front of the Newspaper Building in New Britain I dangled off of)—"the depth charges!" we all yell—"Or is it just a joke, just fireworks!" Bedlam—Great clouds of black smoke spurt with each blast 10 stories high—Me and the two girl prodigies or one grownup girl and prodigy and the male other-hero are rushing down the hall to flee, but I warn them "Have we got our precious belongings?" No—we didnt—we all teeter in thought—then start rushing back to get our precious things (into our rooms like the rooms where I'd lost my pants, as if I had had a Tolstoyan childhood in castles with great sun pouring in thru Versailles Palace windows with noble trees outside)—(near Andover St. of Ernie Malo)—but now we're hungup trying to decide what to save and meanwhile the tourist movie crowds are rushing to the elevators and we join them empty handed and as we "pummel" down floor by floor with floor indicators on buttons I worry about a depth charge suddenly breaking the cables and killing us all—In the general family lostness, here, it's like night Gerard died and the yelling relatives in the upstairs bedrooms and the fireworks crashing outside (ours, sneaked and set off by my cousins)—yes, Nin, young Nin of olden childhoods is one of the girl prodigies, she and I must have thought what to salvage in the general wreckage to bring to the Baileys with us—I must have thought it was the end of the world when Gerard died—Yes, the milling tourists are clearly stomping thru our apartments in a wake, one of my heroes of the Saga has apparently died (Hal? cat?), and we the little ones are working out tiny salvations in the huge detonations of world adult disasters, ah me sad life of little souls come back—

IN THE BIG HOUSE ON LAKEVIEW AVENUE in the Centralville Olden Night there is a Mannerly but the Conductor Young-Mannerly type Salesman chatting with me and waiting for his interview with the Board of the Southern Pacific Railroad which will include Cody and decide whether the salesman ought to be hired and retained—but he's so eager and sadly so that I'm all of the opinion of course he should, who else could sell the samples better and in fact "He's already sold a number of them and is so enthusiastic for his work—Good God why not?"—Also the salesman reminds me of Good Old Jimmy Bissonnette-Emil Kerouac French Canadians of Lowell and I'm all for him, I stand around in the kitchen in my slippers just like in 1928 when Blanche's husband was there in sad spats—"Recommend him him for hiring," I tell Cody—right there at the foot of the hill where I'd gallopped so recently (Bunker Hill) on that Eastward White Horse—Cody just "Yeahs" and "Awups" as usual though in a dream he retains a little more humanity, like a not quite empty wine bottle—The Board arrives to convene: a big official blank and sayless like Wayne Brace, and subsidiary ass-kissing brakemen with no brains. Meanwhile "Salesman Mannerly" has already been across the street in the Old Teachers' Home and even discussed me with some of my old grammar school teachers, one of whom however disclaimed a real remembrance of me because it was so long ago—"Well,"—I say— The board convenes... Cody isn't going to vote one way or the other because he's not concerned. Brace will vote <u>against</u>, as a representative of Management of couse; the brakemen following his suit. I'm not on the board but nevertheless I'm going to make a stirring memorable speech anyway recommending Mannerly for obvious, practical reasons for the railroad (as I'll show) and because I like him as a poor lost human being of the night and might as well help him—but it all ends in a waking daydream and I've only slept 3 hours in 2 fucking days on this fucking railroad—they can ram America up their ass and all rails and iron machines with it—I'm going back to Brittany and warn my fishermen: "Dont sail for the mouth of the St. Lawrence, that's where you got fooled before—<u>ils vous on joué un tour.</u>"

I GUESS IT WAS MY BIRTHDAY PARTY and for some reason like my marriage I was honored by a great gathering of the members of my generation, the scene was in a big one story house which has elements of the Kellostone house on Hildreth when I was 5, and the Gershom Iddyboy house and also elements of Sarah Avenue because of layout with kitchen pointing towards street thru parlor and also the little cottage across the court has Alice Kerrigan qualities but not in the end— My mother's around, may have arranged the party but wont be in it to interfere (Ah Gaby Jean!)—elements of N. Y. of course keep creeping in— Wine, beer, all kinds of drinks are ready— Jim Calabrese is coming, and Cody and Evelyn, and groups of Subterraneans but well dressed and cool I dont even know but heard about the party and come, almost hostile to my fame... Watson must be there, and Madeleine is there— Julien—but the people, the friends are powerful, intimate composites instead of actualities, for the poor brain yearns— Everybody arrives—it is quiet, polite hubbubs as befits the beginning of a party— But does everybody recall my saying "Something that was supposed to happen just didnt happen?"—(I'm a writer, a sad figure) —and without a warning the party begins to crumble—no laughter—bad sign—the Subterraneans just sit embarrased not talking to anybody—Garden is trying to talk—Cody is stony silent—there are arrivals and dispersals, not much gayety or drinking—Groups pull out "momentarily" to hit the bar across the street—It starts to snow—The sadness deepens—soon everyone realizes the party is a sad failure— Sympathetic expressions appear on some faces— Small groups get in huddles discussing the party anxiously— Some girls come to me with condolence faces— Of course I'm not worried because I have already arranged for a small private party in Lionel's pad in a tenement not far in the smow and have already cut in and out of there several times and back to the "official" main party—at Lionel's there's been records, tea, a few girls, Danny Richman, Josephine—but always these heartbreaking composites and not actualities—Cody has been in and out of this side party, like when we flew in and out of Deni Bleu's with Lionel and Danny—in fact Deni is there, has just returned from a ship, has bought (undoubtedly) a lot of the wine and beer and is deeply disappointed, as always—Finally almost no one is left at the party—Such silence and incommunicativeness has existed between the partyists that it's become a heated, shocked topic of the evening among the handfuls of intimate, rapidly-getting-drunk friends left in my parlor—I'm a little worried because all the efforts of my good mother to give me a nice birthday party have gone in vain— Cody rolls up some tea in the kitchen, leaves Buckle and me 6 sticks each sitting on the table and departs (without much comment, that is, he's not involved in my trouble or with any of the people, and I'm not actually in trouble anyway, just anxious to hear Cody's opinion which will not come because even as a composite he has lost his contact with judgments of this kind)— I'm standing out in the little court, most of them have left, took the drinks with them—in the little open court, snowing on me in the night, I gaze fondly at the little shuttered cottage (like neighbors back of Cody at 1047)—I tell Buckle, who's smoking his tea, "This is the little house of my past—How odd that one of the fruits of my being grown up and successful is to have this little house of eternity in my backyard, ah spectral night! Oh holy snow! These mysteries—my father—what shall we all do?" I consider smoking that tea to dig my little house better—the neighbors who live in it are not in at present, an "old couple"—but no, I've laid off tea, it alienates my soul from me "as it has done Cody's from himself"—the little house has old gingerbread eaves, brown, a fairytale house of lost infancies in some kingdom of the past— Sad, I go back to the last drinks, the last guests at my party— I have my overcoat on and sit in a chair, glooming— The piano, someone's at the late, last piano, among empty glasses—Everybody is crushed to realize that people could have made such a disastrous mess of a poor party, not being able to talk or communicate to the point where it embarrassed them to realize...the whole generation afflicted... Up to me comes the brunette I loved, and still somewhat love— She's "Jim Calabrese's sister" or maybe even Jim Calabrese but "definitely not Marguerite," more Maggie Cassidy, sexy, sad, intimate —She is also so strongly Madeleine Watson that I shudder to think of these Names— She says to me, brooding, "Come on, let's go spend the morning somewhere—the party's over, dont be sad— Comfort me."

"Comfort you?" I say with a dawning joy. "How?"

"Just comfort me—anyway you can think of." Immediately I picture myself eventually devouring her in kisses and love— I'm all heartbroken to love her—and grateful—and hang on—and incidentally hastily reprimand myself: "Her family would have liked you to marry her a few years ago—she was in love with you then—You'd have not only her but lots of money now"—"But you let it all go for some chimera about yourself, concerning sadness, and so your party is sad, fool"— Meanwhile June Ogilvie has been in and out of my party, with the Subterraneans, like a stranger, an onlooker—she talked of other things with them—But my intimate group in which Madeleine is included talks only of sadness and is a fine group—I go out with Madeleine, to the waterfront; there one of her seaman friends is on the corner of a pier, goodlooking, muscles, strange long arms—he grabs her and pushes her against the wall and goes into a deep kiss—her hand reaches out to me, at first I think with horror of this "comfort" of hers but it's for the quart of port wine in my arms—she takes a slug, back to wall, thug to cunt,—I'm amazed—it seems I know this guy, too, and yet of course I'm jealous—A minute later I try to push her against the wall too, for a kiss like that, especially so she'll be soft and out-hipped to me just like she did for him, but she resists, slips out, I end up groping at her cheek for a lost kiss—("Damn your dreams!" says Evelyn—) I'm afraid even to ask what she wants for "comfort" and I have somehow betrayed her request, too,—This is the Maggie Cassidy part—her rich parents was the Marguerite Calabrese part—

Back at the party, it's now another day, the house has changed into a working office, all the people are there working at desks, it must be Monday morning, gray skies press in at the windows, it's like the Hospital ward at Kingsbridge for location (overlooking New York) (in "Albany")—My desk is at north end, like my bed was—Wallington's desk south of that, where the Negro Johnson was and also the dying Mr. Kaiser—(was)—Elements of the party are still around, but all at work now— There are brochures, folders,—issues,—now Madeleine is busy, not as dark, working, not as sexy,—mysterious happenings,—Even the Subterraneans come in and out of the West hall with papers— But Wallington is quietly and steadily talking, or dictating, at his desk and isnt confused at all—I've been confounding at mine— I hear him say "We've got to work in love or not at all—" These confident words I see also printed on his brochure which I have in my hand— "WE'VE ALL GOT TO WORK IN LOVE, NOTHING ELSE"—in love, AT love—LOVE— he is preaching this strange thing in a solemn businesslike office and's not even embarrassed, I recognize him now suddenly as a great man, a saint, he is steadfast and almost mad in his insistence on this—and particularly because of my party, which gave impetus to his conviction, and everybody knows it—Great Wallington Preaching Love in our midst, from his desk in Our Office—but at the back of our minds we all know the authorities wont listen, Wally is already some sort of crank in his "Love" work—but I am moved, and wake up in the night full of awe and realizations—

THAT GORGEOUS BLONDE DANCING BARE-BREASTED on a golden stage before the sullen Charlotte N.C. audience, that Zaza-like beauty—at one point she began pulling up her panties, you could see the brown hairs of her Venus hump starting to show between her sensuous thighs so sexy-tossed—Old ladies began leaving the theater in civic excitement, finally even young men rose and held local caucuses among their seats and I even heard some of them calling for a committee, a rope, a lynching—uproars gathered—the blonde danced on, her huge bulbous soft white breasts with pale pink nipple bouncing in the golden footlight glow— I began to cry out "Stop this furor, this is a beautiful woman—enjoy and watch her—never mind your lynchings and laws—Is that <u>all</u> you're interested in? There's life and love staring you in the face, sip it while you can—besides you dont want to harm a nice woman like that—" No one hears me; angry Southerners are shouting with Southern accents and it seems I never knew they were so mysteriously vicious and organized in that—there are rushes out of the theater—I run to the stage door, I run after the blonde who's now put on her blue slacks and is hustling to her bus with her traveling bag—across a field in back of the barracks theater—shaking her head and saying to me "Well I guess it didnt go over in Charlotte—Elmira's my next engagement—I've been on the road with this act for a month—grossed pretty well in Kewark—" and so on with showbusiness gravity and "innocence"—of issues in the real, political world—and she's short, God so tall and statuesque on the stage and so buxom, and here a short businesslike little showbusiness blonde cuttin along in slacks—fast, fast walker, I can hardly keep up—

THEN I REVISIT SELMA CALIFORNIA scene of my 1947 cottonpicking and living in a tent with Bea and child—but buildings all over the cottonfield now, strange brown grocery store-cabooses on the tracks rolling, wide as a real house, lights inside, goods on shelves—for the "use" of section hands—I go across these litters, enter a store, a beautiful sexy brunette says turning to her father "See, all the men go for me"—this after I appraised her with appreciation and said something—

"Alright Irene," her thin Okie-like father says, resigned—I sit inside the stationary bench at the table waiting to be served—I realize she's "Irene Wrightsman" and this is "Wrightsman the oil millionaire," her father—I realize I can come into money with her—

"Do you know so-and-so?" she says to me —"Cousin of so-and-so?"

"Sure—the one—"

"That cousin'll inherit a million in oil—" (which I know beforehand.)

I start to wake up and forget all about her sex to speculate with myself and with them about these millions—(Railroad call, knock on door)—

And that very day I see for the very first time a brown ranch style prefabricated house being rolled out on wheels at San Mateo—right out on the road—and mention the dream to brakeman Neal McGee, who laughs and says, "Well must have been a nightmare!"

I WANTED TO STEAL A PINK WOOLEN SWEATER from the outside counter of a Jewish clothing store across the street from the park—right on the spot where I was when I watched the boy with the runaway horse and loose reins—New Haven, but also the Chicago of Parks and just as I woke up the realization that it was only the real Frisco and the park was just a Boston addition to it—but I grabbed the sweater, just like a can of Spam in the store, tried to fold it under my coat, or in my arms, walk casually across the Montreal traffic to the Park, but as I woke up it seemed he saw me and also that I only dream-daydreamed stealing it—pink, wool, I dont even need a sweater, Edna had a pink one, I had a red cashmere one for awhile (where?)—(when?)—(Barbara Dale in Greenwich Village)—it is the middleclass security of pink wool sweaters I wanted.

MY POOR SAD MOTHER ANGIE is trying to get off a crummy, I see her up the track, she's carrying burdens, she's "followed me on the railroad," it's hard for her with her old legs to jump off the high caboose step, but she does—How short, squat, sad she looks—how long suffering, that now in these last tired years she "follows me on the railroad"—Finally, after a series of "moves," in the night, she's standing by a switch, we're finished for the night—she looks so tired, old and grayhaired and finally weary now, heavier, much slower, no longer bubbling—my heart breaks when she says "Ride ton point, Jean—and dont walk on your poor legs—ride—and come back home." I'm going to "ride my point" to the other end, that'll be the end of my day's work, we'll rest now—worked so hard—my heart is broken, God, by this sad lonely mother you made me come from and by the poor way she used the railroad word "point" with a French Canadian accent and sadly as if talking to her baby—having to use this harsh Okie word under the stress of earth's harsh inhospitable circumstances—Ah Lord, save her—save me —she is my Angel and my Truth—Why does it tear my heart out that she pronounced it "pwaint"—that French Canadian way of using English to express its humility-meanings—no non-French Canadian knows this—

THE MOST INCREDIBLE BEAT DREAM in the world, it's near St. Rita's church, on that street from Moody, but as my mother and sister Nin and I are traveling up Mammoth Road on some kind of train a woman rushes up shouting "I want to see Dinah Shore!"—She, Dinah, lives right up the street, right at the location of that grammar school—in a house—she has a "canary yellow" jeepster or convertible, which I point out to the lady saying, "That'll be her house there, Olivia DeHaviland has a canary yellow car"—(confusing the names)—My mother and sister accompany the woman: but I stay behind in a kind of suddenly transplaced Sarah Avenue house, it's Sunday, I'm the 30 year old beat brother and loafer of the family—"Dinah Shore" is standing in front of her house, and, seeing that I had directed the woman autograph hound to her she says, bleakly looking at me in an "offical" or "Hollywood courteous" way— "Wont you come in with us?" (for a bleary visit)—

"Oh no—I'm busy—" but, they can see that I'm yielding and in my head I've started calculating advantages I can get from knowing "Olivia de Haviland"—So I give in, but in such a beat obvious way, and we go on in—

"I'm a novelist," I announce forthwith, "you should read my book," I say to the hostess—"Your husband is a writer too—a very great writer, Marcus Goodrich." Then the persistent fiction I have that Dinah Shore is really Olivia De Haviland has to break down here and I say "Oh well, of course, yes, you're Dinah Shore, I keep thinking you're Olivia de Haviland"—but this is so gauche—and I havent shaved and stand there in her parlor, she is bleakly attentive, I'm like a thinner younger Major Hoople who really had a small taste of early success but then lost it and came home to live off his mother and sister but goes on "writing" and acting like an "author"—on the little street—But now, my sister sees that I am botching everything so she steps in and in an even more beat awful gauche way begins to try to impress Dinah with a kind of halting Canuck-English speech (attempts at 'social smartness') (and really painful to hear) goes into some speech about how this and that, and so on, to show how really chic she's been at one time, we've been, our really more elegant real backgrounds than what shows (and in spite of this pitiful brother, and she's spoken up really to cover me up and also cut me, as she has her own ideas about how to impress people like Dinah Shore) to which Dinah listens even more bleakly—and my mother standing by like the original lady who wanted an autograph—it ends on this bleak beat note...with me all anxious and chewing my nails—the comic opera of our real days—

I'm also a neighborhood self-styled roué ready to make all the housewives but they dont really want any part of me, except a few of the older ones who want to have something on my mother—

A WHOLE 13 HOURS NIGHT OF DREAMS—I visit "Eddy Albert's" house on a kind of Andover Street, incredibly rich house, also previously dream'd, "Ernie Malo's" house which is of course the Andover, and "namelessly" connected to that dream-house where I'd lost my pants—New Britain, the football stadium, the river, the levee, the Hartford-New Orleans glittering-dark boulevard, the roominghouse I lived in—Eddy Albert's father who in real life showed me a $100-bill is in this dream, in rich Mackstoll livingroom, I come in from Andover street, pause to admire rich modernistic front like Spanish style but simpler, "these people have millions," a great Tolstoyan house of halls and events and patriarchs by the fireplace, I say hello to everybody in that nameless New York which is in Keresky's San Rico or whatever Towers —Gad the Jewish millionaires I've known to whom a thick rug means more than all the Salvations of 2 Billion suffering mortals on the groaning world—the evil intelligence of Bill Keresky! In the Eddy Albert bathroom I pause, looking out, as his sister 'Ricky' (after Ricky Keresky) comes home in an old car and steps out with a pet turkey—very pretty, pale faced, dark eyed, little sensual rings under her eyes—I'm watching, like a masturbator in the bathroom, mindful she'd never dream within this dream I'm watching her—the rich Ricky, I could have her and have millions but she'd never gave me a look and never would (I remember her bedroom near the bathroom when she was 17, 1939, now she must just be a randy old pet bitch of time with a demand for minks turning over whole industries)—but here she's still a young girl—and it's gray outside, somehow raining, like the tragic Andover Mansion—Also, at the Phebe Avenue house there's been a kitty soaked in cement, thought to be dead he was left on a branch to decay in his pitiful cast, but suddenly I saw him try to move and still alive, I cried out, I ran to my mother to ask her to help him, she got a knife or stick to scrape him with, wet him with hot water, he cried from the pain of this, he was supposed to have been dead for 3 days—I tried to imagine who were the beasts on Gershom or Phebe or Sarah who had pulled such a stupid gag—(like, of course, the cat in Life Magazine)—on the green porch where I'd played jockey (stirrups on rail) my mother worked hard to save the little cat —her face drawn in the strain but she wont give up—the cat stirs with life, it's amazing how his little spirit managed to live anyhow—

There were other dreams, sagas of them, I cant remember but these 2 for tonight—they come close-packed in one cunning steady stream from the same fount —I woke up rejoicing in the music of the little birds and had a vision of the Indian squatting in the soft brown land of the brown mountain in the blue sky not Spain but Mexico —prophetic dream of 8 o'clock a Spring morning on Sarah Avenue Lowell—Why write, rejoice unendingly like humble St. Francis—return to New York on foot followed by the children, come to kneeling Irwin and Stavrogin-eyed Julien in an East Side Street—keep within yourself the fund of love and rejoicing, be in your soul the child the same child again, forget literature and English after these next 15 years of Art, and retire to fasting and prayer in the desert and descend to the sweet villages of Man

"MY MOTHER IS PREGNANT" and she'll have to go to Chicago for an abortion so I'm going to be alone in the city awhile and I'm cuttin out of this poolhall on a Friday night, I'm wearing a white shirt with starched collar, and a tweed sports jacket and clacking along like I used to do in prep school and college, at first I take a quick view of the doings of the boys in the brown poolhall, the card tables, then I hit the glittering city night and I'm free to do things on my own for a week or so, and I'm young and happy—

SO I'M GOING THROUGH EL PASO, a clear dream and vision, it's all wild and merceds and shacks jumbled like Thieves' Market and just like it with green shacks, fruit littered dirty mud walks, Arabic filth behind, squatting brown ragged figures, blocks and blocks of it under the clean blue sky of Indian City morning, smoke rising from a thousand noxious pots, strange hidden robes, wild, orange peels, bananas, the end—I'm driving through with somebody and cry out "Look at this wild Es Paso!—the cat told me it was the wildest place in America if you live downtown!—this is sure downtown!"—and blocks to the fore began the skyscrapers of a spectral city but it wasnt Mexico City it was on a plain in Texas and not only that the Texas of raw snow and moons and mountains for suddenly I saw Apache Navajo Indians with their shaggy ponies at a dismal rack, in front of almost buffalo tents in the general rueful wreckage of the market shacks and they wore floppy rider hats stained and rolled by snows of the Texas plains, and brilliant big blankets which also were were thrown over their mournful little paints—the Texas, the St. Joe and the Independence of the Old Real America, dismal, cold, vapors rising from their brown mouths, feeble thin smoke from fires not warm enough, the cold blue keen February morning sky—El Paso of the frontier border, of the Navajos and Indians, of the market shacks and dung heaps and ponies, of the sad Indians and dumps of poverty—downtown wild huge Merced El Paso—I was stoned! I wanted to get off the car and live there, work on the railroad, dig it, like I'd planned—Get <u>high</u>!—

LONG BEFORE I WORKED ON THE RAILROAD, in earlier dreams of traveling down the ribneck Mexican continent, it was always rails—railroads—sad mountains—the railroad, the yellow ground—long sad trips—Now I'm in Mexico City, I go to live in the sumptuous apartments of Bull and June, June is still alive after all—They have rich brown furnishings, but somehow they got hungup to live with a paternal older couple and awful bores, an Okie 40-year-old painter or carpenter, goodnatured but suspicious, mock gay, and a funny type middleaged thin whacky woman with (like Vera Buferd) a husky voice, Tallulah like, sexy—I go into the bedroom with an understanding with June that we're gonna do some fucking, we get in bed together, June rambles and talks, but suddenly the woman jumps in bed too and that brings the Okie and it appears he's not pleased about that or something's wrong and dammit I'll have to leave the comfort of this house—so I never get to bang poor sad June—and Bull is somewhere in the house, silent, isnt interested in those El Paso Navajo ponies of mine—(like when I lay in bed beside June one time in the dark at 118th street on benny and Bull came in and sat talking to us, I guess)—The wacky woman doesnt really want to screw but to create an issue that will get me out of the house, as I long suspected of E. So I'm out in the Indian cold again, and return to El Paso, and walk in the dirty snows with angels in my soul, whoopee! That Es Paso!!

ALL THE GAY LITTLE BALLET DANCERS OF ECSTASY are around—it's the Theater, I'm there, that old spooky opera house and high school auditorium and classmeet hall of all my days, with hints from all the stages of Time's earth and actors too, and behind is all the corridors, props, dancing girls, phantoms, sceneshifters, stagehands, Lon Chaneys, Ernie Malos and Madeleine Poopy Dolls of poor time–I dont know what happened, seats, darkness, lights, crash, events, hooray, blah, wah, went backstage, falling sandbags, the Marx Brothers—if it could have been the twig that was on that white wall, Crist Sakes the buses dont wanta growl fer leaves or let kiddies yell while the record turns and the machine drowns everything out sucking as it goes sugar, spice, matches, ragamuffy dusts—shit! It was the Theater, is was the Vast Dream, too much to understand and cant wait till the day! Phnark!

WE'RE IN FRANCE, Cody and Evelyn and I, driving cross country, I'm in the back of the station wagon on blankets and sheets, the sun shines thru the glass, I say, "It's hot waiting here, let's get on to Paris!" but Cody is at the gas pump, busy, and intends to stay in this rolling part of the country for some time; the Country has Dali road signs strung about, Mutt and Jeff cartoons in the shade, a crazy place, with a central ribbon road rolling over the hill to Paris. But I cant believe we're really going to Paris and I'm terribly impatient. What a dark dream to have in a cold room. In a cold cell.

A BARE BLEAK HILL "outside Mexico City" and I'm hiding in holes, looking towards the ocean for which it is also a strange beach, people come looking for me in the rippling winds—Finally I get a nice bagful of tea and feel it with my hands, smiling—A friend is near—Events—

THE BUGLES WERE BLOWING in a white sand court and I was there with the same soldier who crossed the General MacArthur artilleries of the hospital dream and there's tents,— To the right, in dark stall, we got caught doing something; the hospital had red brick—I might have been wearing a polkadot shirt but more gray canvas and something from the field of elephants that tore up the dust of carnival field, the stands, the night, the people waiting—for the fireworks—I was given a white sheet, or shroud—In the yard the tents, the bugles—we were leaving for some kind of England—they had soups brewing in great stewpots in pig fat copper Kitchens of the Prime Roast of Rib and great omnivorous odor of boiling water so flavored —with beef. But nothing for us, a couple wasters. It had faintly to do with the hill house the other night when I was a child, under pines—not as clear as those original pines beneath a very early morning school of the hill at Hildreth behind where bakery stood—the young teacher, who also, (pretty as she was) had a place with a lake—early primitive woodchips—and later, boats... but I'm just a little kid and I just woke up to the fact of the morning of life—and stand in the yard, dew wet, pink from eraser sun just come up over the school hill, a tot, bleak—I really did watch an Armistice Day parade in the cold red morning from my 3rd story wood porch, crying because I wanted to go back to the woods of all that summer

IN BULL H'S BIG AIRPLANE we're all gonna go fly—he has big wings, a DC-whatever, he takes off from our grand estate near the Pine Brook Woods and off we go—arriving at the Carnival City in the Strange Mexico, setting her down he does without a flaw on the big rubber tires over the black ground, rolls her right in—We have drinks in the plane—A woman at first wanted to put her coat over my seat but I picked it up, sat, put it on my lap, she apologized, we finally laid it over a back rest of the seat, and throbbed and shivered on across the air—Where are we? doing what?—Just a little intimate group of us going up in the plane—The runways are waiting for us—There had been events in New York apartments, we flew off—the place we're landing at is that Mexico of Navajo Smokepots, merceds and sad ponies of El Paso; banners are rippling:- we've come to our business there—it's also the Gen. MacArthur hospital grounds—and Canada—always dreamy weird—place of last night's tents—

WILD AS SEEN FROM THE TOP OF A GRASSY HILL outside town, it's Mexico City, where are elephant water holes, funny shepherds, me with a huge well not huge medium sized bag of tea in which I'm running my hand as though gold but it's just weed, and the day's bright, flowing clouds, the Plateau North of the Great America of the World is fine and white like a beard of a patriarch in the Popocatepetl Sky—my silk and lace-able you—Events—

ROLAND BOUTHELIER is driving us, Ma, me and a bunch of kids in the back seat, from some festivities—We were at a springtime town with a castle and wooden tenements—I daydreamed of living there, in huge rooms of castle, of my sister being amazed by the size of my room and Ma's room—Also I wanted to live in the tenements and I looked up and some of them were abandoned, broken windows, looked burned—(We traveled thru Maine, incredibly sad the land—) I walked around, the grounds of the castle, the town,— In the castle itself was Bertha Fortier Joe's sister all alone there with him and Philip—family gone yelling—and a little Mexican child they owned who climbed up way high on the facade and fell down landing in the courtyard with a tragic plop bouncing on hands and knees on his belly flop knees and I thought "Oh he'll be crippled for life like that!"—like a paralytic swimming but Joe didn't seem to notice nor the Mexican child hurt—he'd just hung down and dove off his perch—Then I asked Bertha for a sandwich, considered sex with her, thought of her big figure on the couch etc.—wandered around the big halls back of the kitchen—The "main" family was gone away on some celebration—Then I took a cab and had to rush to find a lawyer in the little side street shopping district off the hill of Moody—I was on the hill, hailing cabs, got one, big car, in which the driver had his wife or woman with him up front but in the backseat her huge coat and bundles took up all the room and I had to push hard everything over, cursing, so I could sit but they didnt notice—When we got to the show I paid the fare, leaped out, and realized I didnt really know there was a lawyer at this shopping-movie-district, had only heard—There were swinging doors, a saloon, people, noise—the name of some dentist or lawyer on a plate—melting snowbanks in the street stores—

Joe—Roland—O lost—He, Roland, was driving us back to Lowell in the '29 Model T Ford, pretty soon we'd see the dreambrick factories over the pines again—and it would be Sunday—and the Pawtucketville of the radar mystery air raids, of terror—the Royal Theater is dark even right now— My Ma sat in front with Roland as he drove the Lakeview Road which is like the spectral Mexico Road—My father not there—As tho once Joe, Philip, Ma and I went driving alone with Roland—

Pauvre Roland, he's also Cody—It was warm, sunny, earth-springing melting in that Castletown, we'd gone South, the snow was trickling, humidifying, making muds fragrant in the fine air—Events—I was sent for the lawyer merely, wasnt the hassler in dark halls—All this is gone forever. What is the name of our death?

All that we lost will come back to us in heaven.

I'M HURRYING OFF into the sandbank in back of the old ladies' house, naked, dont want nobody see me—I see a bunch of little kids coming, I sit in the sand, buried half to the waist, till they pass, they look at me curiously—Then I resume my hegira in the woods—Back at the old ladies' redbrick place there's been a big party, banquet, Mel Torme was there even and played the piano and I leaned my head eyes closed on the upper keyboard to hear him play, Mel didnt mind, played wild and good on the rest of the keyboard—

STE. JEANNE D'ARC CHURCH the long low basement cellar church on the hill at Crawford and Mt Vernon in Lowell, —gloomy masses, vespers, gray, the kids, me, people—There've been holdups in there, gangs of thugs walk in from various doors with guns and conduct holdups as the priest continues with his ad altre deums and hardly anybody notices except a quiet gossippy panick—I'm there during one, with my little chums, the young men in gray coats in the doors—after (no money taken, nothing that I can see happening) we all rush out to the dark street to chase and find them—they're gone—there's snow, kids, sliding in the gray air—I walk along home down dark Moody, dark Gershom, discussing it, to my dark house on Sarah—everything has that darkness of things buried in the ground decomposing—it's ME—I see my tree sprouting from my hand now, I see Novenber through the bone, I'm waiting for further Springs and blossoms for my black, I'm the Frankenstein of my own 6 foot grave goodbye little golden children of the glee mad world.

WE WERE IN TRAINING—we had to pass under the little plank with our bicycles, everybody made it but me, I couldnt even bend down let alone pass myself or the bicycle under, tho I did succeed to some extent,—"Well this guy's got too many muscles," laughed a sub coach—"Yeh, I'm muscle bound," I said, "I cant even bend—" It's because I'm wearing my big thick wintercoat—and "muscle bound" is the fat around my waist—Frank Leahy seems to be the head coach, the place in Julien's loft, dark—a woman in an old house is looking at us from the window—A bakery Nearby—We're learning to be Secret Service Sneakers—God the mangled impossibility of those 'bicycles'!—

THE HIGH CLIFF OF GREENERIES, trees, buildings, rails, overlooking the down low plain of the world with its pale river and factories—I'm living on cliff, working railroad, they call me for a local down the cliff on the plain, I dont like it—The atmosphere is sad, advanced—

MA AND I ARE IN "NEW JERSEY" on a bright Saturday morning, we go into an abandoned roofless lot, find in tubs a great smoked ham, a box or pail full of living moving white sponges, a crate of pasta, all kinds of food—nobody around—Ma takes the huge ham and goes around the corner to an outdoor sink in the lot and boils out—"You dont have to do that," I say—"Oh yes!—it'll be (cleaner) better—" Meanwhile I work on the other stuff—in the bathtub—pastrami like—Suddenly there's Van Johnson sitting there watching me—"Is this your stuff?" I say—He seems no commentish—In two cottages at the end of the street his own huge mother is roaring mad—It's all the Saturday morning market merced New Jersey of the Navajo Indian El Paso too—My mother and I are tremendously happy, we've found $50 worth of non perishable food, we'll take it home to Long Island—and say "What is this place, a store they started and abandoned?"

EARLIER MY FATHER WAS BACK among the living—very pale—but sure of his own health—and had just got a new job in New York—but I know he's going to die—especially from his face—He's been down to the Union—Meanwhile I'd been high on a great building overlooking infinitesimal harbors, unafraid—The history of the Kerouacs in huge spectral dream New York.

SAD EPIC OF THE RAILROAD, I'm a brakeman, young, inexperienced, working across vast illuminated lands with my bird on a leash—Bird Handlers of the railroad take it from my hand after each trip—I do my work, finish a run which was up in some side country (of which more later)—arrive at end of run at sea coast, get off train and suddenly I lose the bird and it flaps up into sky with leash—"Hey!" I yell—it's happened before, you get demerits—"Where will it go?" I ask the Handlers whose sad work with cages and seed in dark Railroad Bird Roosts I'd never realized before—Maybe I'll find it again someday roosted in a gable still with the leash around its little neck—or in a sand nest of the shore—but until then—It goes into a George Sanders sentimental comedy, he owns an antique store, is a bachelor, a beautiful girl comes to buy something, a romance starts, he takes her to lunch, makes her a gift of one of his expensive doodads wrapped in a box (a present 'before lunch' and which to me seemed irrelevent)—his partner fetches it—and all the time you know someday George will re-find the bird—but he seems reluctant to continue in such a sentimental movie and tho my heart thrills, my spine shivers in the hope George Sanders will find his bird...he snuffs off the idea and is already displeased with this script and his part in it and you know the movie will not be a success—somewhere in his antiques, in his store, attic, loft, in the sadness of the dream, the leashed bird will reappear, the brakeman epic youth of George Sanders be roused up again—tears—The illuminated land to which the railroad ran...a man was driving all of us in a car, to a picnic, he swung off the road and over a double track for a shortcut but with a dead end curve so that you could never tell if a train was coming or not and tho I'm just a little boy nevertheless I worked long enough on the railroad to feel obliged and also licensed to yell 'O dont ever do that! it's the most dangerous thing you could do—find some other way to cross the tracks!' and everyone listens respectfully even my father, Pop, who might have been annoyed that I yelled at an old friend of his but they know and respect my railroad knowledge and nod and agree but suddenly I see that around the curve the doubletrack ends at a double deadhead block so it wasnt dangerous at all and I say "Oh well then it's alright, I thought—" and down at the station meanwhile trains are loading, arriving and departing—We're having a big picnic,

I'm under a grandstand in the rubble finding lovely fresh apples, fruit of all kinds for Ma and especially I want plums for her but only find one but a good one and bring it all back to her at the sand picnic very proudly and she thanks me—It all is during this time the bird is becoming mine and I work it—till my work leads me to the shore, and the loss—I see it fluttering weakly in the sky with the heavy leash—gray skies

DARKEST NIGHT ON THE COLUMBIA CAMPUS corner Broadway and 116th on the Barnard sidewalk, no street-lamps working—a dim mist of rains—shadows passing—by my peanuts I stand waiting—warm April night—mystery of the West End Bar, the corpus in the Hudson, Edna in a Russian darkness over the campus—I'm almost afraid of marauders in this gloom, look around—Timeless the world waits—I wake up—wondering—

JOE AND I ARE RIDING HIS MOTORCYCLE, I'm sitting ass back, heels of my new crepesoles dragging in the Southern town street—I want to ask Joe to slow down so I can turn around but he doesnt hear or care, it's Rocky Mount or Kinston, we cross the railroad tracks and go out and go speeding over the countryside but suddenly it leaves us and a great gap of nothingness and sand hundredfoot canyon yawns beneath us and all we can do is fall but Joe has that wild crazy hope the wheels'll stay upright which they more or less do, we ride the saw horse, at the bottom is a dry creek, another climb up sand steep bank like those we tumbled on Lawrence Boulevard *nightmarish* vast waiting—a little house shack occupies the opposite slope, we go in, a beautiful girl named Ann Buee or such is living there with her Ma—has a tape recorder, books, is lonesome—I go in there cockdangling naked—I start talking to her, Joe disappears, I have to go away to get money or work but I'll come back and marry her—she is honey colored, innocent, sixteen sweet—cluttered bedroom—sad sandbank sunlight fills her eternity windows—

Earlier it was the Lowell High School football practice field in spectral outside-Lowell—Tewksbury Road—Coach Keady—Kids of team—me coming up—from sand hegiras to Boston—it's too late I'm too old but I still wanta play of the kid team and those imaginary jumping up and down Billerica hills leap into Lowell suburbs like motorcycle hill and Italian fountains of Frisco—the honey-hearted girl lurks for me—Milk!

GREAT SAGAS that begin in my Phebe Avenue yard with I'm in the Army and soldiers are resting on the backs in heavy rain from full exhaustion—they haven't got all their gear yet but nevertheless have been sent out to hike and exercise some still in just pajamas—same applies to me so I hide in huge hospital house, tell myself I'm waiting for my gear—Many beds like dorm at far end—I go to mine —No raincoat, nothing, just my pajamas with a big hole in the ass,—Pat Fitz comes to visit me and reminisce about the Army—I desperately figure ways of sneaking out —return to railroad in California under cover somehow—relates this dream to old Navy bootcamp madhouse dreams of regimented life I hated so much—

SUDDENLY I'M IN "NEW ORLEANS" down on the piers, hundreds of ships, thousands of people walking cobbles, I go to Acapulco lines and ask for a job, he asks if I'm union, I say "Used to," doesnt hire me, he asks if I'm union, I say "Yes," show him papers, he hires me—I sail as handsome ship's officer with blond hair, map shows our route down Mexico East Coast—At Frisco suddenly all the wooden houses and hills—I want my Ma to see them, too vast I'm being rushed half awake through halfbaked dream tho at New Orleans a great sight: walking in one tight melted together but stiff group Scandinavian ships' crew officers in front men and maids in back the short ones in back walking against tall North Sea tweeds of tall others, swinging Nazi arms march from consulate to shore, shore to consulate, grim, glad, I catch fleeting glimpse of blondhaired cabinboys with golden hairdos gathered in buns at back—wild health of the sea and Scandinavia—

CODY AND I ARE COPS working on top of a steep frightening pyramid like hill where some people cause trouble and we send for 2 more cops—as they come up they can see me sitting writing in the cab window, Cody is down the hill, I think to myself "They can see my uniform, they know I'm a cop, now they'll find out about me, this is my first duty"—the hill is clear, high awful, I'm afraid to look down at all those worlds but here goes...

NIGHT OF MIRACULOUS DREAMS March 16 Sunday night —There had been a national catastrophe, it was announced over the radio at gray rainy dawn, it was riot of so great proportions it was some kind of revolution—over "police brutality"—bandages were strewn in the street—people had revolted against the police—survivors were stretched out in annexes—announcers were grimly announcing everything in quiet voices on the dawn radio—I knew something would happen when I went to bed the night before—this would change the course of history, America and the world—no school no work—Like days when I was a boy, rain, I'd stay home with Ma and see before me sweet hours of playing with my marble horse races and papers and as in Gloomy Bookmovie in Sax she'd occasionally look in on my games, bring cake, milk, fresh pies, show socks she was darning and <u>assure</u> me it would rain much too hard for this afternoon too and so like the national riot catastrophe now she cant go to work (if so I'll walk her to the bus, there may be bricks flying—but it's a good idea not to—but she insists, "I dont wanta lose my job, it's the only security I have")—

Then there was Lowell, the Gershom street house, Iddyboy looking young and thin now that he's in his 30's came rushing in in a white shirt, with Rudy Loval—I had been all around the world and away from Lowell, I was back, with Ma, in the 34 Gershom street house "Hee thee Boy!" cried Iddyboy joyfully so glad to see me—sweet sun and flowers outdoors of a Sunday morning everybody Pawtucketville going to church—Rudy Loval as ever eager, warm—this is the happiest dream of my life—

Meanwhile:—There are visions of the Lowell Sun Sports page, stories about yesterday's Red Sox game all the lost players with their names intermixed, Jim Piersall goofs of other times proving that the future is every bit as rich as the past; also there are old stories of me writing sports articles for the Sun curiously intermixing the triumphs of 16 (athletic) with the workaday tragic job of 19 on the Sun—somewhere there I took the wrong road—I left Lowell in March of 1942, to go to Washington—returned (after construction job in Pentagon, and Jeanie, and throwing gin bottles over the moon) in May or so—and ship't out to Greenland—on which ship rough seamen who saw my child's soul in a grown up body broke my spirit by spitting and cursing at me—and in October 1942 the ship sat in New York harbor and I tried to tell Archie Sleepyhead Hainesy that I was on the Columbia Varsity and he didnt believe it, so 2 days later I was back at Columbia practising for the Army game—but was staisfied enuf—and left that too, again, disgusting everyone, for to go to heaven deviously I had to cut and dodge institutions, plans, schools, formalities and be silly—and in Xmas 1942 I came home with a radio under my arm to rest, but the war took me away in 3 months and drove me crazy—mad—in a madhouse, they stroked their chins seeing me write—the book was The Sea is My Brother and it was a dreary attempt at Naturalism with a sea background—When I came home again, June of 1943, with Navy clothes on my back (for my original clothes'd been sent home before they shaved my heads and all our heads and that is why the police riot was so great, such emancipation)—now Ma and Pa—my love for my father is greater hidden—now it was New York, they had a little apartment over a drugstore in Ozone Park, the druggist's name was Sam, there was the Old Piano—my mother'd brought it from Lowell at great expense, my father cursed but loved her—like George Burns and Gracie Allen—now no more Lowells, no more rainy days of no school, but cities, sodomists chasing me, girls and women who tried to run my life. The—Town and The City is not yet written. It must be written again. Irwin Garden was right. So M—but also there were voyages, to California, lying on the ground, to Mexico, walking among the whores to the desert, the peotl and the t, to San Francisco of the endless green night—all for nothing—I was back in Lowell, Sunday morning, the birds singing, and Iddyboy in a white shirt thin and handsome and the father of four children whose picture was in the paper and Iddyboy look't different there but it was him and all children are gorgeous because they are the beginnings of our evil, make golden foundations for mountains of crap our later years multiply and ferment our early childhood years are not years at all but a sweet outpouring of eyes—Thus Iddyboy also beautiful look't out gladly at the world for the Love of God and his wife was not in the picture she was in the background somewhere, I was ashamed in the midst of all my roaring happy friends of heaven of succumbing to the sexual invitation in public of the girl or woman who wants to prove that men are not priests—And they are not beasts, they have bodies wild and hungry upon the golden rod of their being the flesh wrapt around—homely—Women have folds of milk around the depth of their womb—and let me think of the best the most beautiful—It is not fair for anyone to accuse me of not loving women—least of all myself who knoweth—that what I reach in the woman's heart is thru her flesh and she misconstrues the idiot child to be the monstrous beast—Around the world on ships—and swirls of that behind me—, my attempts to understand the world on every level it has—and so Iddyboy and Rudy knew without my saying all these things—and greeted me back home with cries of joy—"Gus and Lousy and Scotty and everybody knows you are back—They'll be here soon—" My interesting little backyard is still there, I can see it through the back window—from the depths of hell I know that I can make willful confessions of evil but in heaven are wilful hopes of God's good love and this latter is what I choose, Genêt—poor Jean —my brother—In the newspaper in my joy suddenly I see my picture in a baseball uniform wearing a pitcher's purple jacket, squatting in a 3rd base box, cleated foot, hard brown athletic profile,—apparently I'd been a star in further dreams than this one of actual conscious life and activity—It is only when dreams lose their importance that the dirty business of evil begins—by dreams I mean what you saw in your sleep—not what you wished in your day revery—Carloads of Lowell guys as usual were driving to Fenway Park in Boston for the ballgame that afternoon—Irishmen—I read stories about the Red Sox—When Cody saw me in San Jose in the kitchen with his son on my lap he shuddered, I saw his hand quiver, his eyes were wild, I never saw him so glad—This is almost Iddyboy and

Rudy—We start gabbing and talking at the kitchen table the round big one, Ma's around, putting up new shelves, talking to her own kind of neighbors again—we should never left Lowell—but now we're back and everything saved again—

BUT THE DREAM HURRIES AND SHIFTS—I'm in Baker Field Columbia in my football uniform practising alone, I sprint 80 yards dodging in the heavy suit, my legs drag like lead,—that was another mistake leaving football because at the expense of just a little physical weariness I could have convinced everyone that my heart was in the right place instead of this writing which is so dangerous to my sanity—so that I may have to stop soon and just work on the railroad in the dark—No coaches, nobody watching—I go into the showers and change—some of my old team mates are there, no ones from the freshman class wonder who I am—they dont realize how old I am—and that so absurd, the coach doesnt even know I'm back and would take the uniform off my back—I am temporarily secretly back on the team—Ben Wirt is there, contemptuous—on a Main Street in Pennsylvania he once squatted and took a big crap, crying—he was drunk—talk about your Sinclair Lewises—he wore contact lenses—he used to cry and curse trying to catch me on the wing around KT79 run—I had to squirm out of his reach to get by and make my way down the field to the goalposts of reality—The Coach would laugh—we were all tired—The big game came, crowds roared, behind the grandstands secretly I ran up and down in my stolen uniform hoping I'd wake up—I walked down the steps of the 215th St. El with Cliff Battles, at the bottom step I dropped my milk bottle, this is how I almost made the Columbia team and they said I was another Cliff Montgomery proud name—now they'll say I'm another Wm. Blake—

I'M ON DARK MOODY STREET with Billy Artaud, I lend him 50¢ and a book, as agreed, he walks off home without a word, I yell "Okay Bill?", he doesnt answer, I say "Hey!"—no answer—and panicky I suddenly realize He's mad and means to keep book and 50¢ both and never return them—he is striding away, his face is red, his ears burn as I hurl curses at him and run after him, he disappears in his house—on the street I'm yelling at the crowd all my grievances—

SOME KIND OF LYNN... I live alone, around the corner from newsstand Mainstreet, I'm waiting for something—There are girls around—cats—I have a transom on my door—I make lunch, and go to work—Up on top of the Fellaheen hills overlooking the sea finally I live in a swank expensive cottage with Peaches, now I go to school with her with my prepared lunch but something is deceitful—like we at night we make love but she holds a piece of steak to her cunt and I have to come into it on the edge in the slit she made so when I feel my cock throbs in spring pushing thru the membrane of the silly meat I can well tell the sham but she in her childish daydream insists—by day we sit together in the same double bench in school and it seems the whole class is expectant of our lovemood, when it's good the class buzzes excitement and accomplishment reigns—when no and I slump in my seat... tenseness, waiting... A famous guitar worth $1350 or more had been given to me in my Lynn bachelor transom days (very like the transom of the Mel Torme old lady party)—(redbrick etc.) With this instrument by day on the sea hill I gaze at the sea, waiting—I go down towards the village, a beautiful middleaged Fellaheen Flamenco woman sees my guitar, disengages herself from the women washing at the Pawtucketville hillbottom creek—comes over—she too lives in a hilltop cottage with her old man—I say "How much is worth?"—"You wouldnt get more than $350 for it"—She starts playing it—it is a great guitar—her playing is so gorgeous my eyes fill with tears —a little boy so high also listening also stares up with tears—her hands work swiftly so swiftly and magically at one point she lets go and alone the guitar continues a shower of heavenly strums complicated rich according to the arrangement she prepared with her magical knowledge and technique—I am in the Fellaheen Land of the Great Guitar—there are pale hills—dusk—the even star and her saucer cup moon make bright couple in the keen pale edge of oncoming blue—I am happy—I go up to the hill cottage with the woman—she feeds me huge meals and so when I go up to school I cant eat my lunches and the man in the seat in front of Peaches and me, a distinguished middle-aged New York manabout town, gives me a lunch bag saying,"You left your lunch in the seat yesterday"and I realize with horror I been eatin so many big meals—etc.—and the whole class is wise, all except Peaches—it's only when I wake up I begin to think "I gotta make Peaches realize this steak is silly to give me herself not a piece of meat"—So huge and timeless, the events strung out from some intenser center and forming vague distant points only to be found again when centers and universes shall shift in other dreams—

BRIEFLY,—I HAD TWO CATS in Amsterdam Spectral, little yellow bouncer, bigger gray, kids with me—I go down the street looking for the tragedy which is somehow related to that pregnancy of Ma's when I clacked out the poolhall—the moon—I hear noises, I look back, Good God a great commotion, a huge thin Giant Hound is bounding across the street with my cat in his mouth—I start to run to stop it—I know it's too late—my poor personable kitty is gonna be dead, my little Bouncer I know <u>it's</u> already inside that Baskerville Beast's throat—O from where came this horrible canine of ghost? ? ! !—I scream as a huge bus balls by—I hear my child weeping inside—I pantomime in the street at jeering men looking out the back window that I know my little kid's in there, I make the signs, they laugh, but a stern woman inside prevails and has the bus driver stop—it stops—it has baggages like airport buses—the plate says QUEBEC—I open the back sidewell door, jump in, ark, loud and foolish, "Is my daughter in this bus?" and as I ask I realize I made a big mistake and was only paranoiac and though they're all (except stern woman) laughing a dead silence falls over bus as no answer comes and it's in the negative—and my little daughter of course delusionedly is somewhere else not here I am crazy and realize it and all they too—So I step out and back—that's when I look up the street and see my tragic little cat in the great dog's mouth—my children helplessly screaming chasing it with its long spindly ghost legs chiaroscuroed against dreamdark horizon of Amsterdam mothswarmed—

THEN I'M IN A LUNCHCART—record store narrow, with gang of friends, 2 uniformed doormen come in, I give a Chaplin military salute goofing backhand to brow—but suddenly 2 real cops rush in—we have T—I sneak out door unnoticed and rush down street in back of George Wicksner and caution him and we hide in doors and I really beat that rap—he disappears—I go (halfworried about fate of friends in store) into a beat bar, a blonde whore is sitting on floor facing wall, I stoop and hug her and put cheek to cheek and she says "Just that, just that, nothing else"—she's been wailing blearing crying at whore wall of dark sad saloon kicked beaten—"Just hold me like that please"—we are heroic Russian lovers in a hovel—but suddenly she starts stretching and spreading legs on floor, says "Hmm," snuggles, says "I have prick trouble, man," and I say

"How much?" "Five"—"That's too much—how bout 3" "I cant"—I wont give five—I hold her—she lusciously stretches

MADELEINE AND I are in old James Watson apartment, I'm sitting on couch in corner, suddenly I look and she's taken all her clothes off, has perfect little hourglass shape and black Italian cunt and I jump her to the floor and start right in eyes closed elbows to each side of her ribs pounding in an elastic strange box that stretches as tho my cock was stuck inside pajama pants urging out, which it was—(as I awoke)—and all Madeleine did was talk sprightly and little girlish as I worked wordless—In Montreal I dreamed something and woke up sneering at the ceiling—about "the deception of the female"—making horrid gesture with hand at hole void of red room in Ste. Catherine bordelle—Also other nightmares of drink now forgot—and no Montreal of runaway horse parks—how strange reality of the bleak endless world which has no destination or meaning or center and the sweet small lake of the mind

RIDING IN A CAB with friends and Bob Boisvert, talking about Chaplin—when we get to Harcourt office Bob is saying that sometimes Chaplin comes in solemnly in dark glasses or sometimes tips his hat gayly his homburg smiling and Bob walks off thru the office to do something pulling a little wagon and I follow turning to friends doing that tipping gesture to explain how-Chaplin and jump on wagon and ride it thru office goofing (like a young Chaplin) as office workers stare and Bob doesnt notice or care—At a rack are various big Pages covered with current publisher's cover designs and photos, I look at Scribner's for GO but realize it's been already published—Did this woman upstairs kill my cat? No, the kid's back and has it hidden like he used to do—poor kid—

I'M AT THE BEACH with guys—Julien—suddenly I see Al Eno and Albert Lauzon, God how Lousy's changed, fat puffy, he lisps, has regressed to a silly precocious child, he sits on my chest and tells me what's happened since—only the other night I'd seen him in front of Destouches' store—Swimming in the beating waves we'd had a big ball, it floated far out, I went out to get it—Later I want to show 2 of the guys how well I play mambo drums, we're in a house, they wait as I rush out to get a proper drum, a kettle—I practice 10 minutes by myself in the street to be ready—I play well, my fingers race and rat ta tat—then I go in but en route find an old broken real drum and try it but it's not as good—by the time I get in the house they've lost interest and left the parlor where we talked about it—semi Phebe St house, semi by the sea—

I'M GONNA GET A JOB IN THE STEEL MILL, dark horny iron pieces are taken out of an oven and somehow slatted up on a long bar and poor grimy ghost has to lift that bar to a horny bier hot, everything hot, with hot clothes he pushes against hunks of iron and somehow pulls slat bar back and disposes them—I anxiously wait my turn to start this work, fear's in me—I see now they have a gray gloomy iron treadmill will bring the steel to my feet, my slat-bar—not only impossibly heavy but red hot—experimentally in this hell I lean over the bier counter to test distance, it too is hot—

I have a sexy Italian girlfriend on the little street tho—we neck—people are off on a trip—so I go buy her a halfpint—of whisky—cause I drink wine—She has hips—Earlier a group of phoney literatteurs with Dick Beck-Ed Williams cultish cool manners have me visit them, hint at trips, advantages—finally allow as they'll let me join their organization and announce it gravely and impressively—I'm afraid to ask what it'll cost me—and afraid to tell them I dont want to join anyway—"I never join organizations"—The 3 Negroes that tried to run me down in a car are somewhere out in rain, driving—"Only last week we came from Montreal,"hints literatteur darkly, "from the Northern Boulevard we drove in"— Ah that poor bleak hell mill of horny iron doom

I'VE BOUGHT A TICKET ON THE S. S. EXCALIBUR sailing from a hilly Mexico to Havana so I can see Bull who is there—I go to the ship, see my dull brown lonely stateroom like the ones in doomed Dorchester—one of the officials is queer and is trying to rub my hand beneath the desk so I look down there and say "Hey there's a rat down there!" feigning innocence—The ticket is high price, I learn the ship's also going to North of New York in all kinds of dream gray ports—it's sailing at 12:45—Meanwhile I go home to make a lunch, get ready—a stone's throw from the big slip and ship—I'm completely alone, I sit and daydream how I'd tell the story of the queer steward to Bull and others—I decide not make a lunch since there's three meals a day aboard ship—Suddenly I realize I'm late and have no decent clothes—sweating, my legs dying, hobo pack on back, I'm hustling to my house, uphill, downhill, to get remainder of my gear—big whistles blow—I see the ass end of a ship passing a pier—I rush to the bridge, it's going very fast, <u>it's my ship</u>, I mistook 12:45 for 12:15—Oh the world is sailing away and not a sound—I watch from the bridge but it isnt the Excalibur, I realize I was correct, it's still 12:45 sailing time, I have a half hour but I cant see the Excalibur in her berth any more—I dont look long but rush home struggling to get my final tomatoes and pack them—I take a shortcut and get hungup on unnecessary steep hills—a funny sunny hilly Mexico like Frisco—there is a golden silence in afternoon naborhoods—I dont know what's happening—

SOMEBODY'S GOT A HOLY CHALICE of some kind in his hand and just then (calis!) (caw-<u>lis</u>!) in a mirror we see someone—impersonating the Devil—from the rearview —and the chalice, having a Cross, makes the Devil hiss & shiver back—

EXCUSING MYSELF FROM DINNER I rush up to make a scheduled phone call—The colored girl is watching me from her bedroom door—as soon as I finish the call I rush into her room and we wrassle & love & soon she's on my lap black & naked & I'm working up—then I turn her over to her back & we work—ecstatically madly, gladly—I wonder what the people downstairs will think of my long "phonecall"—

ON VAN WYCK BOULEVARD before it was built—CALL ME MADAM or some such show has been a big hit, everybody's talking about it, I see it (marquee)—walking home, I see a telephone pole climber with spikes go running up a pole and start snipping at wires, amazing how fast he climbed, little kids watch awing—A thousand things happening up and down the crowded Boulevard—I'm blasting, curse cause I lose an ash—I find a sidewalk in front of a house with a thousand pretty little decorated stones in little boxlike places—I steal six or seven, carry them in my hand, drop one under a car bumper, recover it,—My mother whom I just call'd is come to meet me instead of waiting at home so I blank butt and suddenly across the street we see a popping fire racing and snapping out of the ground along the gutter—a car follows and drives over it for fun—fire goes right through a pole and traffic light and on in a straight line thru pavements of a big intersection—"It's the telephone power!"—A happy dream full of life—

GUY GREEN AND I and Marguerite standing on corner of "72nd and Broadway"—to show her how a guy does, he falls over in a tremendous fall landing on his side on the pavement just missing hitting his head, comically—on the raingrit cement—people stare—but I am suddenly remembering something I missed or had to do or have to catch and just as Guy hits the sidewalk and Marguerite's laughing I take off sprinting up Broadway like a madman and without a word leave them there—I say to myself "People will think I tried to outdo Guy's fall." Later I start down a dangerous incline but feel it's safe because it's dry, a dry sidewalk—but it turns into a rack a hundred feet high, I try to hang on to my nervous cat—I feel he'll do better by himself with his claws—a crowd is watching—I throw him to a beam—he claws wildly missing and hissing and hits another one and tumbles off and falls to the sand way below—(like a rollercoaster at the beach)—I cry—I'm afraid—I can't come down—Later I'm sick—in a house—back from the hospital—events—people swirling around—why don't they leave me alone—etc.—a mixture of wax images, real blood and sad floors—

DRIVING THRU SPECTRAL LITTLE CANADA with Easonburg Annie and Ma and Nin in back seat, and me too, Annie is asleep or drunk, "Put on the brake!" I yell —"you stupid sot"—she doesn't know where it is—I dont either—I reach for the wheel, guide the car swerving and crazy over sidewalks, inside lampposts, around corners, other cars, hospitals, canal, night—I aint worried, I do well from the backseat—Later Good God I'm walking with Nin and Ma in the Textile Mill alleys back of Prince and Aiken and Ford and Cheever—dark, cobbles,—that old dream there—Suddenly we see a grim dark little man, "It's Dave!" I tell myself joyfully—Dave Orizaba the Mexico city connection—Nin and Ma are terrified—"Come on!

dont talk to that man! Oh!"—but I rush up, only see it's not Dave just an old greasy hat ghost bum of Lowell alleys—but he has a package—tea?—he follows us, and the fleeing women—madly I reach back and feel his package, it's solid like meat no marijuana—

BROOKLYN—strange sad scenes haunted with guilt, that began long ago at the age of 4 when I FIRST went to Brooklyn with Ma—Now it's the grownup LATER just as in a dream and I'm trying to tell Ma if she takes the El and gets off at Juralomon she wont have to spend so much time gettin to work—She worked in a shoe shop when I was 5 and we lived on Hildreth in the Kellostone and when we took the first coldnose trip to black New York—something there is wrong on that end of the line of life—also the Marquand girls are around—the work is towards the Park, the Island, the Ozone, sunny haunted Els—of old dreams—Ma Evans Lynn-haunted redbrick house, still—Ma and I are on the street waiting for buses, it comes around the corner but doesnt stop but a halfblock further, we run after it —I remember Denver—all, all haunted and mixed up—Wesley Martin is much much clearer—There was a girl, hauntedness, guilt, nakedness—shyness—her sister—a lost dream. Earlier at dusk in Columbia South Field I'm heaving in long throws to two kids but like in a dream I wont and cant get em off and wind up and run and never let the ball or rock go—till later—when there's no more force—but I high hard em in good at times—Where's Edna? Jule? Franz? and Pan American Bull? What am I doing in San Luis Obispo? rain—no raincoat money—that's what I'm doin in San Luis Obispo

RAILROADING THRU THE SAN JOSE MAZE of tracks with some kind of Lil Abner Indian buddy like the baggageroom Indian in Frisco—and he has a buddy himself who is all gold, we go downstairs to a crowded meeting basement hall full of poor workingpeople, there's a party of some kind, a ritual, something they dont have to do but do it anyway—Indian's buddy is wearing tights and performing on a platform, I think "If any non Indians walked in here now they'd think it was a queer party"—Indian and I are doing the Railroad Company a favor—"Guys like you and your buddy are one in a million," I tell him, and mean it, as we leave to go back to our Engine—At one point I'm on my knees mopping some spectral corridor with that red tile floor like on old passenger cargo ships—We have rods, clean out the engine, go down steep nightmare grades—At one point I'm on the Centralville Hill trying to crawl hands and knees down a steep hill and rack—argh!—helping ladies—My Buddy is like Iddyboy, Lil Abner,—like yesterday's fireman on the Guadaloupe Local—The San Jose yard looks east like that lost Bunker Hill of the White Horse Riding East Out of Frisco From Cody and Evelyn in the Market Street Cafeteria—commence, finis.

MY MA HAS ACHES AND PAINS, I tell her to take a little whiskey to ease it,—a minute later I see the old man sneaking out of the house and going to the drugstore—for aspirins, those same old aspirins—I'm mad, I tell Ma again, she pretends to brighten up "Oh, whiskey?—then what do I do?"—"Take it with aspirins and go to bed"—The scene is somewhere in the East, sad—

Earlier it was Pete Menelakos greeting me on a Lowell corner, begging me to come back to Lowell, it's the same impossibly warm Lowell that doesnt exist (I remember cold mornings of oatmeal and hostile school)—G.J. is with me, & good old Scotty—I tell Scotty about himself—G.J. is friendly,& anxious—It is now 8:30 A M Sunday morn in San Luis Obispo, pristine & bird-sweet—O Lord what shall I write? how bend these sinews of my art & on what anvil? what harp? what frosty window Beethoven hope secure? what SEA draw? and the mind inbend?—Pete Menelakos who was there in the Moody Street saloon the last time I saw Maggie Cassidy and when Moody Street was still thus named—in fact when Lowell Sat nite Summer was one great riotous scene on Kearney Square of bus waiters for the Lake, shoppers, dancers hurrying—up there in just one corner of vast America—now TV-itis I think has ruined the culture cold—

IRWIN GARDEN—somehow always a vague aura of murder around him—a Manhattan pad—a long talk—his finger up—I had gone to bed with the first clear vision & definite message of the necessity of my death—I'm walking on a bench among crowds, it doesnt matter that the scowling stocky muscular man of 30 should die—one of two billions on the dead bilious world—with its burden of time, tedium—Woke up realizing sex is life—sex & art—that or die—

GOING THRU A WORLD OF SAD DEBRIS as a train—myself a train, the front of one—down some track—thru plasters, dusts, whole blocks & plazas of disaster & wreck & junk & cellars—Finally I start hiding in this junk—in broken cellar rooms—I go with my mother to the shoe factory to collect her Xmas pay check, there are signs on the wall, one of them says "Angie's Son is Back From California"—I feel tremendously insulted that those people assume I just want her money—I picture her gabbing happily about my imminent arrivals—Slaves in a shoe shop, slaves on a rail, James Watson made a tragedy of the the day Town and the City was accepted and "Frankel" rejected and now he has 20,000 dollars to my one—Gad, what were those broken Roman cellars—?—along what Lowell canal route—They ran right straight by the Y—along the Boston & Maine tracks and out to the Princeton

Boulevard yards where Joe and I explored old locomotives
in the 30's old pots of old 1915's rusting in the weeds—
The old sad plaster of haunted houses of Lowell, the
cellars of the Rat beneath gaping no-more-floors—the
horror of the death of a house and a family once in it—
a pristine leader made it—lost it—has none of my sympathy

LIKE NOTRE DAME in Montreal is the Cathedral, the
church that the train of some sort is pulling into and I'm
with Bull—a giant dog runs alongside in the aisle, by
pews, it's the "Hound of the Baskervilles"—Suddenly he
takes off impatiently into the air, becoming a giant black
bird, and flies over the altar and descends at the vestry
doors where hurrying theological students pay no attention
to him & he lands upright on his feet like a man—&
humped with wings walks to a vestry door looking like
Satan, black, sad, but also like a humble vestry janitor—

Later I'm with Bull and some youths, I
say to one of them "I look like a hoodlum too when I'm
dressed sharp"—He doesnt believe it, looks at me, an
older jerk talking crap—I feel silly—

Ah so our bird is tripping into a vestry
door—behind altars—

I woke up, looked in the mirror with disgust at my fattening oldish face—the giant bird limped—
the kid who looked at me with suspicion was Don, was
blond—(Don Johnson I met in Mex City)—

That limpish Angel Gabriel sooty bird—

ROLLING ALONG THE SIDEWALK in (it's the place of
the mambo drum practice on sidewalk) New York subur-
ban downhill sidestreet on a little toy wood wagon affair
I come to two children, boy and older girl, and with very
few pushes make circles around them and then give them
the wagon—after which the little girl wants to go into the

house with me, I say "You're too young" but is she ever pretty!—and really not too young (urgh) in India—I give her lil brother the wagon—I go in the house, upstairs, talcumy eternity mother bedroom, waiting for Evelyn—"O—she's not here—it's Friday—she's gone to see Cody at the hospital"—I wait—soon the little girl comes knocking—I debate with myself in the masturbatory master bedroom—Earlier I'd seen that little girl with Raphael Urso at the beach, foot of low cliff—the Lakeview Avenue beach on the dump—gray—they'd told me to wait for them there, they'd be back—it's the same eternity dump of my first view of the world from Lupine Windows—the Merrimac Sea—tic tic tic—

THOSE AWFUL AMAZON WOMEN of Rome have got me as one of their slaves dancing in their torture chorus, a ritual, in the Circus—people watch laffing, clapping—the sexual dance—they'll stick you with a spear if you dont dance—the big brunette runs up, grabs me, pulls me, makes me do lewd suggestive stuff with her, all a formal written dance but I'm a reluctant slave, unhappy paramour—the crowd roars glad—it's also a kind of basketball floor, the St. Louis Parochial floor—

ME AND THE BRAKEMEN are playing catch in a lot,—for fun I make sensational catches falling softly on my face, diving around, over my head, backhands and backhand backthrows, all with a flying ease—what a ballplayer I could have been!—if the professional A&P's hadnt been so grim and anxious!—the tall brakeman, Mulles, Bostrell, Schaefer, amazed, makes me hard throws—still I stab them, impossible—finally I miss one—it saddens—in vast quiet the force of the sun is burning out, dusk birds sing—up through the vast tree we see rays of gold, and smoke—I throw the ball up through the hole as immense music plays slowly—The old conductor's putting in his last report, the day is done, the train is done—This is the way the world will end, in rays, red, people watching, silent, tired—The world of the mind is the real world—the rays of the mind the real rays—

I'M CARRYING LITTLE LUKE or Little Tim in my arms, little children of the spectral gray Liverpool hotel after some offense of some kind are clawing around my body trying to reach up and tear him to pieces and so while I hold him high there he is sucking on my nose—The women are around but there's a big fight, a riot, a big plane had just took off from Cow Field–night—I hold the baby, turning, struggling, he blithely goes on sucking my nose—

THAT CRAZY HORACE MANN Jewish kid—a great wit—in my dream past it seems I knew him—he was very wild and interesting—I was at a girl's, a Jewish girl's rich New York apartment—he came to woo her sister—she didnt want him—but he spieled—amazing the things he said—I got a few letters from him—I knew his funny father–but so many things were happening in those days I hardly had time to answer him and after awhile abandoned his correspondence and friendship in the press of events—in real life I never knew him—except a composite of Mussleman in the nuthouse and little fat wits of Horace Mann—but this one was clear, powerful, real–the mind invents like God—He was a sex fiend–he spieled sex to the sister, in such a way she couldnt accuse him–and too fast and too complex for her to understand—I'm there thinking "What an amazing guy–Someday he'll be a producer—I should be amazed by the Eternity of his huge funny complex soul–" Marty Churchill, young Blatberg—Ah inescapable–

I'M HAVING AN AFFAIR WITH A COLORED GIRL like that heroin girl in Frisco—I work in a kind of bakery, where she is some kind of supervising office girl—the hours are long—part Crax factory, part Lowell Hi School machine shop in the basement, part Rocky Mount Mills—part, too, some dream garage like Blagden's on Back Central street where I parked cars—gray, dreary, like Lowell vocational schools on raw drizzly days—She lives in the East 70's not far (in N Y) from where Guy fell down to impress Marguerite and I ran—We—it's about 4 A M—arrange to have a fuck—but linger over something, like heroin, and by the time we come to the door of the joy room she has to go open up the bakery, 5 A M—and it's not she doesnt love me, business and circumstance compel her to leave—(she loves me, she loves me not)—

DRIVING IN TWO CADILLACS one a '52 one a '47 Limousine, with a gang of friends—the driver is Jim Calabrese-Mexican kid—we're going Lombard St Frisco and part Lowell, go down a very steep hill, stop all to get out and buy cigarettes—Lousy, Guy Green, lots of girls—Jim is smiling—We went over some canal—Later I'm back in the West Street cottage with Ma wondering if the organ is still in the shed—Not the family that followed us "in 1931" but "the one after that must have sold the organ"—"the Chalifoux"!—seeing gardens of Montreal and Rubens beyond backyard, so glad—Relishing the roomy rooms, the yard, porch—whiteness of cottage, the old Aiken Street First Street dreams of Centerville—walking in soft dark dusks—by Presbytère—evening on the rosy porch—Good God where's Pa?—Say Pa, say Ma—forgot how to say Pa now—will forget Ma, will forget Mer, will be grave merde.

I'M WALKING ACROSS SOME PARK, there are children playing, by fountains—one lil girl stops me in a copse, says "Mister will you tie my buttons on top?"—she is about 7 but with little breasts or a breast, it seems—I am dark and lascivious as I look at her, her honey color, the little body—I start to tie her top bottoms as she talks —I am going to try her innocence—I feel guilt as deep as the sea—I wonder if there are any mothers around—I prepare to kiss, or take her to kiss her little thighs, gently but right on the cunt—gonna be careful not to tip her over—she vaguely senses my intentions with a blithe blabbering smile—I dont move—I am old.

Who am I?
STAVROGIN

I'M IN DRACUT TIGERS FIELD in a drizzle of rain or sleet, I go to the part in short right field where a spring's welling and bubbling in the snow and wait there for a sign from the shroud of Arab eternity who is going to give me the secret of the frost, on a tablet of ice—I'm amazed to see my old left field tree over which Al Roberts'd hit homeruns and myself once hit one, 450 feet—All Lowell is shrouded on the horizom by the sad sleek murk—I've just come back from big adventures sailing thru tropical canals of the South—

EARLIER IT'S THE RIVER SHORE, the great ship tied to it, I've got a tall girl, a short girl and a colored girl and I try to make em all—I take the colored girl and tell her "Let's go down by the river and I'll show ya"—Somehow the house of dreams where Gerard died is nearby—the Gangplank to the ship is level over mud shores and wood piers, I dont use it as all crew files back ghostlily but jump to the ground and up on pier, ratwise—I recognize members of my crew in the zombie parade—Ladies and gentlemen and then I'm in a moonlit yard of long ago winter schools maybe in the Highlands– pigtails—lips—

LATER I'M WITH BULL telling him I shipped out and sailed thru the Panama Canal—I tell him he ought to ship out—but I cant picture the work he'd do on board and certainly not serving officers' mess—or dishwasher—There's a dump outside illuminated by great sun and Saturday Morning whipped by great winds, along a night's river, where in the vastness of structures I've been climbing around in truancies so elastic that the river changes to a sea, with surf,—the dump changes to a gigantic construction job with me running under stationary and also moving lashed-together pipes—and my hookey-from-school becoming a great coastwise swim with my own human arms and legs from North in Frisco to here South in Bigshore Spectral, a guy watching me—O south City of my Dreams—and Shore of Oceans—my throat aches to find my way back to the place where I am mourned and I cant even remember any more where that is—

SHOTPUTTING THE 16-POUND BALL in some gym where also there's a ditch, a Chinese kid is trying to sleep on the floor, I tell a big Chinaman "Hey get him out of there I'm throwing the shotput"—Like Parry O Brien I'm facing to rear and swinging clear around—Another kid tries it, exclaims "Hey! it improves my distance!"—There's also a huge pile of my writing including self written newspapers commemorating myself and my novels, with pasted pieces of headline—such a sorry mess of scatalogical absorption it makes me sick—A whole bunch of guys have been visiting me in the second story of this wooden I-think-seaside house, Nin's been there—now they're waiting for me downstairs, at the car, to travel, and I'm cleaning up final matters such as my muffcap instead of baseball cap, khaki jacket with fur collar—"Aw go on out there with just a shirt and breathe in the cold air!" advises Irwin Garden excitedly—it's Maine—I'm writing myself to death —I have so many crates of crap and paper and writings I find an original typewritten copy of a novel the carbon of which I'd been working on, thinking it the original—poor funny sonofabitch.

I'M INVESTIGATING A WHOREHOUSE in Mexico City or Paris, I walk right into a courtyard and go down between windows, screened, seeing inside the round buttoxes of Negresses reclining with magazines sometimes eight whores in one little room—My buddy snickers at the entrance—Then I'm sitting on the shore house porch with Maggie Cassidy watching two whores who are standing against the rail watchin and waitin to be propositioned, one of them a brunette with imperfect features, the other her fat ugly pal that you have to buy also, like girls in the sailor park—the brunette applies rouge and suddenly looks much prettier, her eyes and eyebrows stand out exotically like Indian beauties of Organo Street—I look at Maggie, she is unbelievably cute with her rosiness and dark hair and eyes like black agates—"Maggie" I say, the whores pretending not to listen, "this is one of those times when your eyes are black"—Maggie is interested in digging whore life and goes on chewing her gum in rapt absorption—

WALKING THROUGH SLUM SUBURBS of Mexico City I'm stopped by a smiling threesome of cats who've disengaged themselves from the general fairly crowded evening street of brown lights, coke stands, tortillas—Unmistakably going to steal my bag—I struggled a little, gave up—Begin communicating with them my distress and in fact do so well they end up just stealing parts of my stuff, I dont want them to take my shoe tree, (Ed. note: Shoe shapekeeper) one does take a piece of metal—We walk off leaving the bag with someone—arm in arm like a gang to the downtown lights of Letran, across a field—I feel it's because of my betrayal of Ennrique Villanueva of Vera Cruz who'd given me a rabbit foot which must mean something to an Indian—the Indians are mild but dangerous—I cajole, feel hemmed in, losing my "belongings" in the real world and have to become crucially involved in it—

WE GO DOWN INTO THE UNDERGROUND SAND CAVES of India, me, two women, a boy—there are Burmese snakes, idols—we get lost and cant find the opening to get out—It's all near Lowell-like sandbanks—purple eve outside—

LATER I'M BACK LIVING AT WEST 20th street and I'm sitting at my writing table after some friends have left, writing in red ink in a large flourishing hand the final lines of Doctor Sax and suddenly I realize Irwin is still there, still awake reading on his cot in the corner—

ON A SHIP IN THE CARIB we go zooming 60 miles per hour down Main Street of a town, Georgie the Polock says it's Santa Rico, Porto Rico, but I cant believe it because the houses are American, the signs in English—I claim it's Galveston but suddenly we see the KEROUAC HOOK AND LADDER COMPANY—Outside town on the black sea a great boat rowed by fifty Negroes is alongside, they're hardy young singers who want to come on board—I want to get off—Georgie says "I seen em before, they're all young and well built" —I think "They ought to be with that rowing"—"Galley slaves of song"—That town was really Kansas City Kansas—

THE UPSTAIRS BEDROOM WITH THE BARE BULB BURNING, on Gershom at Sarah, the scene of BROTHERS

KARAMAZOV, a pale pimply thin ascetic sickly John MacDougald is with his be-stockinghatted father arguing, they have a half gallon jug of Tokay—Cackling craftily the father asks him over to the bed to adjust his sheets and suddenly slowly unfurls a folding sword of some kind and slowly playfully slices gently on John's brow till even it penetrates and cuts the brow skin a little—"You crazy old fool Karamazov!" I think—In a rage John picks up the halfgallon and throws it across the room, hooking him right in the face and the old man crashes down bloody and dead off his bed—Downstairs in the lobby of the Gershom Hotel there's excitement first about some fire of disturbance, then about the murder—I walk off to my house across the street—

HUCK AND IRWIN are staying with us in the Richmond Hill house, they're in my room singing Jewish Hymns, Irwin in a high Quavery synagogue choir voice, Huck a huge bass—Irwin's just found him a job as waiter in a synagogue home—Huck concludes his song with a big socko showbusiness finale bass, heard everywhere, while I'm washing my teeth in the bathroom—Applause—Pa's in the livingroom—There's been lots of people at the house all weekend, including, earlier, Vinny, GJ, Scotty and Lousy as of yore and it's NOW and I'm telling them about the railroad and in a great epic poem and they listen to the New Zagg—Later I do go to work at the Boston and Maine Yards, Lo!—Shaggy Northern Indians in dirty striped robes are gathering the lettuce waste in the pile field, their sad dark women are walking off all clinging to one another in the coming winter wind, O sad!—and it's right down the yard over the heaps are the boxcars, there's the brakemen stepping off, looking for his sign, I have to go up and ask where my local's made up at—Also men Indians in the middle gathering the junk and waste—I say to myself "Ah, not only California Indian section hands, but the weirder one of Home and North and this iron ruddy loss—"—The big weekends at home at 94-21 have included Rachel, people, big tree shades, just like in New England in Lynn, that's why Pa was there—O I wish humanity would come visit me like that, I wish my dreams were true, I wished I could work on a railroad like that—it's nothing but the same Boston-to-New Hampshire-to-Lowell one I've dreamed of since so high—

A GREAT HEGIRA OF MANKIND IN AMERICA has crossed the wilderness, is almost in Washington but the recently martyred revengeful Indians are close by and coming—It all began somewhere in a theater, I was there, in a seat, there were girls, eating in booths,— Now the great parade goes over the Potomac River bridge into Washingtom as just then the Indians upriver dive in the water and swim it—"They're going to surround us on the other side!" —Some of the bridgecrossers start popping the Indian swimmers with rifles, some women shoot—the swimmers are suddenly not Indians but ordinary people trying to reach the same shore—I can even recognize a girl who'd been in a booth with me in the war land—I see someone aiming at her to shoot but changing his mind—Others do shoot, the swimmers lean their head into the water, floating drowned—Suddenly also at the safe end of the bridge great crowds of people are hurrying in the shallow water along the bank, apparently further enemies, one well dressed man throws his silver dagger at the bridge as he walks under—it goes over and down in the water on the other side right near himself—the masses all melt, the war is confused, we're all rushing pellmell into a new peaceful life, the river made the difference of the war—or the difference of war—So now my mother and I have a little grocery store on a drowsy street in neighborhoods, one afternoon I go for a walk under the shady goldgreen trees—Five blocks up in the New Orleans-like drowse I suddenly faintly hear her "Deni Bleu!—Jacky just went for a walk—he'll be right back!"—By this time I have a seven foot salami on my shoulder, it's shaped crooked like a twisted branch, I struggle back to the store gleeful with this great weight—I pass the same girl of whom I'd been so bashful in the long-ago booth of the war places, I'd been left alone with her temporarily and I remember, I wouldnt talk or look up—I come into the store, Deni is thin, he jumps up as I make a <u>hey</u> face—"Who'd you think it was?" he cries shaking my hand—"Want some salami?"—and as my mother laughs Deni starts on the salami but suddenly he starts shaking olive oil and vinegar on it with the frantic action of a kid jacking off and spill pints of it all over the floor—"My God not so much" my mother says—"Oh I love olive oil!" he laughs, and smears his mouth with it, glad—I gaze rueful at all my oil on the floor—Anyway war's over, (this was dreamed and written July 26 1953 Korea Truce day)—

JULIEN DIED—we have him at the wake, we the subterraneans, it's Julien's house on lower Fifth Avenue but our wake, it even gets in the paper and it's mentioned how Dick Beck's antiquated stationwagon always parked in front sprung a leak and flooded something and he got a summons—Julien is not on his back in a coffin but sitting up on a chair in the corner —everybody talks and drinks nevertheless, even gayly— It's also Gerard and my house on Beaulieu Street and sadly brown—I remember going in there the "second night" of the "wake" after having seen the television program announcing Jack Kerouac reading Children's Tales and after long interminable horrors and sorrows at Pennsylvania Station's marble corridors waiting during hot holiday weekend nights for trains, around johns, getting in trouble with the cops, inexplicable, sad—I see Beck's car out front, go in—The side door is open but also the vast front one with its blinding apocalyptic spotlight and I go in that one eyes wincing and bashfully crooking my shoulders and sticking my hands awkwardly in my belt as though anyone might think I'm taking the second night of Julien's wake lightly—thus I shamble in, he's still in his corner but this time in the freedom of choice I dont look—the kids are sprawled around, I sit on the couch with Roger Barnet who shows me a clay bottle of Gin and Gypsum—GIN & GYPSUM—"Should we drink it?"—"Sure, I would." The girl (Shelly Lisle's wife) already has her glass and ice cubes ready—the wake had much gayer been the night before, now the publicity and the seriousness of Julien's imminent burial begins to weigh on us—Irwin's somewhere around—How still is the grave displeased youth of death in his festered corner chair, how solemn, still unyielding, still disapproving, priggishly prim, mort—

SUBTERRANEANS AT A JAM SESSION in the Open Door, which becomes a great theater and I'm in the cellar trying to figure the way to sneak in free, I see a giant stairway without steps that turns out to be an escalator for the theater employees and I say "All we gotta do is climb that, jump up"—"But no" says the kid with me, Dick Beck or Lisle or Gerard Rose, "you've got to show your goddam pass and badge at every door, at the top of that escalator—" it's the big eternity Brooklyn movie still—We see a few of the employees, their heads motionless rising from the vast punchclock cellar of Lon Chaney and St. Louis Bazaar 'Sale' Hall gloom-prop backgrounds of screen and stage, to the plush lobbied heights—one an ordinary Negro workingman—There are jam sessions, wrangles—girls—cops—Later I'm at the beach investigating a historic landmarked famous old cottage and in fact so old they've only bothered to put two or three notes at certain places like in the pantry, by some old moldy cups, a note—I vandalize and bust up the cups and think of tearing up the notes—It's just an old house and moldy and small—I'm afraid to go in swimming because of the same reason that foodwater was charged the other day, as if radioactivity of disease—not drowning I fear but some nameless salt sediment of disease in the mud of the water itself—It's like spectral Lakeview beach on the side when I got that Pale Sun Sunburn of WPA baseball days and the ancient beach of Gray Glook Lake where I refused $5.00 to go in swimming (age of three)—Danny Richman with me at the cottage which is also like the wrecks and ruins Ma and I found Pastramis in, in New Jersey—the "Van Johnson" time—Later I'm eating in a restaurant (after a namelessly long night at the Fortiers and my mother saying "They never make us a place to sleep" but the truth had been Mr. Fortier'd arranged my bed in a middle room on this "Sarah Avenue Fortier house", a big double bed but Donnie was in it—Bill Tenor's Donnie—and immediately was on me and what with Ma in the front room and the Fortiers in the back and Nin and all the lights on and the closeness of all the walls and the aversion and horror I felt and Donnie loud and crazy to blow and jump all over and strangely like Joe I rushed out to find another bed to sleep in which was when scene changed to gigantic upstairs rooms empty and gloomy like rooms of Salem Street Manse)—in the restaurant (after submitting my Cortons porkscraps to the contest Cook who slopped them into a big pot and prepared them as I waited anxiously by the sea outside his kitchen) —I go in, aint hungry, sit at table with owner (Johnny the Bartender) chatting (and like when Johnny was "in France" in that other Restaurant-by-the-Sea Dream) and in comes that awful blond hooknosed brakeman of the SP from Frisco whom Cody hates and thinks officious, he sits down and orders coffee and as soon as my friend the Owner goes off to get it leans to me trying to borrow money on the sly (which I aint got) (and owner Johnny notices and rushes back smiling to avoid hassel for me) but the brakeman serious, intense, in a low voice trying to make me understand—It's also like the restaurant by God the very restaurant of "Aunt Anna in Maine" dreams and part Washington D. C. when there was a glittering boulevard at night like New Hampshire avenue and sad scenes where I wander looking for Big Slim in the soft impossible mystery, courtyards, the marble insides of spectral hotels, stadiums of roar, river levees, corner bars with shirtsleeved men jamming to the door, New Orleans in the air and rumors of the vast alcoholic America which also I saw glittering in the Pomeray dream of the Stolen Mattress and the rednosed son of the wino—The meat of my Cortons Pork Scraps was in great big gray lumps—When for a second I fear the brakeman is going to order Cortons or Johnny smilingly offer him some for lunch because I know they're still hot and have to cool in the refrigerator, I see the confident smile on "Johnny" (whoever he is) (Roland) who knows all this perfectly well (about cooling)—Ronnie Ryan, Buddy Van Buder, the whole world swims by, archetypical as plots...

I'M MARRIED TO JOSEPHINE and with all her friends around in the kitchen she makes fun of me and my "writing", I'm there with all my manuscripts, gooping—a cuckold paramoured to a dike—I make up feeble stories and try to write them or act them out with disinterested friends—Later Ed Buckle or Buddy Van Buder comes to try kitchen window, sees me, says the publishers want another novel to look at (a falsehood, what he really wants is a jolt of heroin again and I know it)—a bleak laterlife with no balls, no joy, no Ma, no Kerouacism, nothing but the possibilities of the present ripened to full horror —without any of the charm now apparent—I'm like old Uncle Mike in the cubab tears of afternoon or that incredible teary old Canuck lush in the Papineau Tavern in Montreal who cried when we carried him over (called him over) and I was amazed to learn this lonely broken heartsensitive wretch was one of the richest men in the neighborhood—people avoided his big Weeping countenance and frank blue breton eyes—he was the one said I should drink Caribou Blood—Le Sang du Caribou—something Breton & Lost—

LUCIUS BEEBE IS USING MY ROOM in the first floor apartment—he has his son with him, as I'm preparing to go out for the evening and taking a few things with me like razor etc. into the adjoining room to ablute, his boy is already retiring in the sack and Lucius who is not the real life one at all but is supposedly Beebe but shorter, friendlier, a visiting dignitary from Shmolorado etc., he's in his undershirt shaving—I go in my side other room like Huck's room of the other night and discover I have to go back and knock for something I forgot, which I hate to do—"By the way you do know Manley Mannerly in Colorado" I say—at the door—"No"—"Why he told me when you're in Denver he takes over for you"—"No, not in the least, dont know the man"—he looks like Mannerly—Earlier I was journeying across water and New Orleanses of Sadness and up along the roarsome lonesome Mississippi with populated shores—some kind of great blue bay or gulf, my hands cupped over the wave to see—Doomed to travel always in America, road rail and waterscrew.

BIG HORRIBLE ACTUAL EXPERIENCE of hot flaming death, end of the world cataclysm comes and hits New York disintegrating all buildings and I'm standing around waiting for it to happen and for how I'll feel when it does— It does come, I'm standing in a New York courtyard, the whole city and everybody is swirled to the right and as if flattened and whirlwinded out of sight in a searing mass like the collapsing house in Las Vegas flats—Doom in the air so awful, people'd been talking about it for days, now suddenly rumble the visitation arrives in New York and everyone's in ecstasy-anticipation of the actual final stroke of death—Everything disappears in disintegration, I with it—but my consciousness doesnt seem to disintegrate—

GIGANTIC SAND MOUNTAINS of the railroad, a hospital or big brother infirmary nearby, the sun, a yawning cave pit—I say to myself "I knew I was going to work on the railroad again, but I'm afraid really afraid I think of these sheer drops, peaks, trestles,—" The rails lead into sweet All Lowell laid out below in some March sun, in fact here there's the daily noon move to clear the mainline for the hotshot passenger to Boston, I see the ancient conductors and proud young brakemen of Lowell in blue uniforms jabbing in the breeze by the engines—I'm up in the sand cliffs seeing this, working freights—Later it's my writing desk, typewriter, paper, novels—I uncover the old Cannastra Finistra paper roll of Sal Paradise ON THE ROAD novel—I'm talking to a man and a woman, she's going to Mexico, is a parent, says from now on she's going to really live and enjoy genital sex, there's something vaguely futile about her as though she'd been making big final decisions like that all her life—selfishly like me— the futility of the Bohemian decider and undecider trying to find hedonistic formulas to happiness in an ascetic ball of globe covered with unhappiness—In the sand pits there'd been a hegira of adventures with my mortal enemy who was trying to get me to fall but b' god in time after time of clever formula and slow painstaking ah-bedeardoed acti-vishmity ah done laid him onerous bones and all on his rack and pit pot bottom plot, aint never seen him since, 'ceptin I remember his face, sad figure on hill, distant hostility like something in the wind, sadness of his pinpoint soul dementing to me like a rock thrown from the universe of light—but as I say I succeeded in somehow avoiding him and making it and now I'm alright, I had to struggle through all such horrors to get to peaceful railroad securities—It's the shroudy stranger in a white B Movie serial shirt—in his earliest Lowell Lineaments was Fish—the kid who punched me—

I'M IN RUSSIA among the teenagers, in a little sort of candy store—I've journeyed far, this is really Russia, nobody knows—"Wow! what will they say when they hear about the Teenagers of Russia!"—There's a colored kid with a funny Raskolnikov visored trolley conductor cap and crazy Russian hair sticking out, he's the hipster of the gang—There's a neat redhaired kid in a buttondown sweater just like a kid in American Hi School—There are two girls —It is dark, cold, thrilling on the great northern street outside, chimney pots smoke—The kids jabber in Russian as I in the eternity high dig them—I go out, in the street I find a beautiful carved ivory switch click knife and put it in my pocket proudly—I will tell the cops I found it in Russia—In an uptown bus I sit next to two Russian ladies chatting first in French then in Russian about the Underground as they notice my darting eye—Finally I arrive and return to Maine to great family reunion, the Baileys, Ma, Northern Maine Pines, everything.....

Russia's young hipster with the stovepipe

Raskolnikov Trolley-visored cap is a Negro like La Negra of Mexico, now 14, or 16,—his hair sticks out and down from his sooty hat like straws, like a "Mardou" wearing a trolley wiper's cap in Russia with a whole street behind her, only an excited boy interested in girls and Russian weed—

THE GREAT SHIP AND ATTIC OF THE WORLD where I am with eyeryone else, all of us like children in white nightgowns—I have my post in an upper part of the rack where the old wooden rungs are falling out, I rush up there to find out what I've done wrong—My buddy Scotty Boldieu has disappeared—and done something wrong—Everyone is sitting in a sort of classroom, en jaquette—I dont understand what's happening but it's all serious and lost and the authorities seem lax and cruel to leave us wandering around in this rambattered hulk and old lost all-pot no one to chide us or complain—I really dont care or know what this place was but we—somebody—

I've come out of the hole with languidj—

THERE'VE BEEN BIG EVENTS & family reunions in New York and I got $1000 from the publishers at the same time I was offered a job selling books in a company car and some other job with it but I go to Mexico to "start my homestead," by bus—On the bus are Halvar and Peaches and their little ragamuffin blond kids who cry and play with passengers and are neglected by their parents as suddenly I'm dozing somewhere "near Kansas" and I hear a commotion, the bus stops, I go on dozing but wake up finally just in time to see the little boy is brushing something off the floor of the bus near the drivers' clutch handle, brushing up grit, crying in a strange emotionless strangled despair inhuman unreal & short, just one cry—apparently he's puked and this stopped the bus and his mother who's been in back seats talking and playing guitar with people is letting him clean up himself far from helping him—I think "No wonder he puked after those pickles and those shmickles at noon and God knows what he had this morning (what his foolmother gave him)"—While we're stopped Hal the father all blond and white has stepped out to pee, he too is unconcerned, and now as the bus is ready to start up again he steps back in arrogantly down the aisle floating digging all the ladies with a perfectly defined hard-on in his blue slacks sticking way out and he knows it—I despise him—I think how he thinks I'm going to Denver again on some other fiasco plan but I'm only "going through to Mexico" I think proudly and I wont even give him the satisfaction of knowing this—of course we havent talked at all on the bus & suddenly I despair and want to go back to New York and <u>take</u> that book job and park my car on Wall Street while I'm picking up my samples and sell my books to my "driving student" clients while I'm at it, and make it, take care of my children if any with concern not like these conceited useless Hals and Peaches but it's too late, the bus is almost in Kansas, we've been traveling for days, hard, slow travel and trouble—even if I cash in my ticket at Kansas I'll have lost $36 and the return fare will cost $36 and leave me $80 and it's all a stupid big fiasco, and there's Hal with his egomaniacal hard-on flouncing down the bus-aisle—The world is drearily repetitious of itself—

FOR THE USE OF LITTLE CHILDREN DOING NOVENAS a railroad bus parked in front of Ste. Jeanne d'Arc's, I go up and ask the attendant if I can get a ride back to Boston on the train bus (it's one gray big coach car)—"Can I deadhead to Boston in this?" He wants to know where I been working, it takes me a long time to think and say

"Watsonville"—He's skeptical a little—I show him papers, old deadhead slips—Inside, the children are praying.

THE GREAT GRAY HOTEL OF THE WORLD, all night, with Bull, Irwin, Ricki, Subterraneans, Gaines in jeans and beard—Gaines is walking along the esplanade in jeans and full Bohemian but also Third Street bum eccentric beard, still having his income money for fixes—At one point a big skid row woman is seen going down the Canal Street with him to a small hotel—The big gray hotel is also a school, I have all my paraphernalia and cant find the class and wander around naked and innocent in basketball courts, among wrangling crowds—It's one big dormitory, there are hints of sad Columbia Livingston Hall dorm rooms in September when the semester's begun but I'm not even enrolled —In a corner room I find Ricki, we go out together, coming back she walks off to leave me the cab driver—They tell me she's run up a bill—I count the three singles in my wallet and decide I cant do it—The house boys jide me as I walk off "You shoulda paid that cab fare, boy, her company's just struck oil and she'll start goin out with that other guy just in time—ha ha ha!"—the bellhops and pimps of eternity —I dont care—I go up, to Bull and Irwin in a room, during the night Bull discovers I have a sensitive nerve in my head at rightside back skull, he touches tip of it—"Now I understand why you hesitated and grabbed your head last night when those people—" referring to earlier dim events—I feel my head, the nerve hurts—Bull is proud that I am so beautifully sensitive but warns me of danger from this n nerve, I can die from a blow—or wrong contact—We're strolling on a great ramp in Atlantic Gray fog, right outside the 10-story of 5-story windows of our room, the three of us—Bull talks in loud voice, Irwin shushes him pointing to open hotel windows—"Oh, <u>really</u>," says Bull annoyed "what on earth do you expect them to hear, my dear"—Later there are some Subterraneans in the room, they're reading my manuscripts, I'm a discovered genius, Irwin is telling them how on Saturday nights of my heroic writer past I'd grab my head from the great inrush of ideas and sensations, it seems I told this to Irwin myself—The listener is Gold from Frisco, who make cracks—Another, blond kid is there, Don Johnson, halfawpedly listening and sometimes commenting—it is a great hive of conversation, rooms, studies of all sorts, absorptions like Ricki's in whose room are elements of the old Upper East Side Elevator Apartment dreams, of her at 1946 or 1947—Meanwhile Gaines has done something funny and once again we see him going down the esplanade in jeans and Augustus John beard, loaded—

I'VE GOT TO ESCAPE AGAIN, the Javert Shroudy Stranger has come after me warning of my arrest, it's a gray bleak landscape in California leading to some impossible Africas and out-of-town suburbs with little black-trees—I have to quit my job and run off—The boys are having their phoney paper revolution and are practicing at the radio microphones under the ramp of the overhead drive—I go to Erie N. Y. which is like the sad port I inquired about ships at, this time there are no blond Scandinavians and shipping but sad people plowing plowing up and down sidewalks that made me topple and a huge railyards like in Montreal at the foot of the steep hill street—"I'll hop a freight tonight, go south, get away for good—he'll be watching the bus station"— Everything unspeakably sad and continuous—

THE LITTLE CAT I HAD IN MY HANDS that had such a sweet sad little funnyface with gray eyes and finally spoke to me in a pitiful little voice, like Gerard's, "J'aime pas demain" and I said "Moi too mon ange!" and felt like crying, like when I heard Ma's voice over the phone yesterday in the New York restaurant, my heart was moved just by the sound and loneliness of her voice, I'd left her alone the whole Laborday weekend and was calling at the last minute Laborday night to say I was coming—that piteous note Gerard had, from her, and which is in my own voice when I address little names to my cats—this kitty was an angel, and spoke the truth—Also there'd been parades around Irene and I in bed, June Evans and Bull, June giving me a half-full bottle of rich tokay and pouring a glass and spilling on bed, and Irwin with Subterraneans out on Paradise Alley sidewalk in Russia talking to a Kosher Patriarch Golem, and Raphael Urso necking with Irene every time I looked away and she saying to him, indicating me, "These old guys are peaceful to be with." —and I'm tremendously jealous, she's already told me to leave, it's dreary strange sinister and about to Fall—Finally there I am waking up hitting Irene and Raphael reaches for me and I grab him too, it's a drinking nightmare again

AS IF IN LIMA PERU but in Lowell up on Lilly Street there are indignant Spanish fathers, scenes in a dark street, a flat, something to do with a murder or rapine, in a high bleak lonely country of the night, I come down from there heading "back downtown" followed by strollers of hornrimmed intellectuals who'd been seeing the show up there with me (it's the same locations as the Great Tolstoyan Dream), ahead are the lights of the Boott Mills on the river, and the bridge—But at Lakeview and Lilly I say "Damn I'm gonna dig my old scenes" and there's Scoop's Store and two blocks from it I come across the house I'd <u>froidly</u> completely forgot, a lil bungalow at present time has two sons repairing roof and yelling down to mother in the dark but in the past was unmistakable scene of Ma and

I visiting somebody, when I was an infant—elements of the Gerard-Died bungalow and the John MacDougald and Miss Wakefield bungalow and all the bungalows—I believe so strongly I'm (not) dreaming I find myself at 35 Sarah Avenue and jump up to dark windows in snow and a baby starts crying inside, next door "Sure enough just like I dream'd" there are Christmas lights in the Alice windows, but blue ones—That lil bungalow was scene of death, brownmothed kitchen, ancient rheumy eyed old Sax ghost place of Lowell Old all smelling of Cubabs & Pain—

BUSRIDE WITH IRENE down Moody Street across the Moody bridge, I turn to talk to the young passenger brakeman, where the river is, is a giant railyard reaching clear to its intensest center at the White Bridge Falls—there'd been a flood earlier—but now, milleniums later, the riverbed is a rail valley—and so I ask him "Are they hiring brakemen?"

"No!" he says emphatically and immediately I smile my radiant smile and cry "Oh but they sure are in California!" and it's understood that he's about to say "But this aint California" and all around in the clear air of lost Lowell I can sense the exciting railroads, the redbrick alleys back of the Old Citizen, on the Canal, outside town in the sand hills, in the river bed—then the sad people gathering under iron clouds in Kearney Square nights, the sad darkness of the old Lowell Sun lobby where in looking for familiar faces and fumbling around I worry and wonder if anyone knows I'm in town—and that Chinese Newspaper Mystery on Schultes' corner, my revisitings in October so brokendown—La peine dans l'aire noire, the pain in the dark air.

While I'm thus talking to brakeman Irene, colored, sensing herself colored, is fidgeting in the seat and as if to say "But why are you talking like this? What railroad is that? What is this Lowell up to? Whom am I anyway?" and all her sundry fidgetings in the public car of the world...

A BIG STRANGE WAR has broken out in America; about 400 or 4,000 Prisoners of War in a camp break loose and burn their way down the Mississippi towards New Orleans —the whole country gets panicky, mobilizes, it seems to me to be kinda silly, it's that old gray war again only now right in our own country—I go down to New Orleans in the general upheaval of war, at night in the great spectral glittering city I arrive at the boys club to meet everybody and there's Cody!!—and he's suddenly given up family and responsibilities and spiritually fallen apart and is a drunkard, a wino, red face and broken nose, tragic, dirty, young-old—I'm so astounded by this change and yet I think "He must look just like his father now!"—Dave Sherman, others spectrally are there too—cardgames—We three go stay at a guy's house, queerlike, John Bottle-like—he doesnt expect us but that very night is having a big queer party and we are welcome—At the piano sits one of them, tall, dark, pockmarked, with a malformed hand, whom I address as "Hands" in requesting a tune and get a dirty look—We're in jeans, young, the queers seem to dislike us but I dont really (in retrospect) believe they could have—and meanwhile those tragic Prisoners are fighting their way down the Mississippi leaving their dead and diminishing in numbers with every skirmish, every new broadcast—I feel sickened by the cowardice and hysteria of America become so blind as to misrecognize the freedom needs of imprisoned men "Communists" or not—the great pileup of arms and pathological propaganda on them—and Cody is battered, nose broken, fired from the railroad, a hobo, Cody Pomeray in his inevitable final American Open Spaces Dempsey Whisky bottle Night as always I'd dreamed of him and of myself—But now it's a serious reality and I realize Cody is going to die of wine and neglect—He doesnt talk excitedly any more but is silent like Okie—Later I go into my livingroom after a long sleep and my mother is sitting there with the furniture rearranged and some of it missing, bare, dark, sad, I say "What are you doing?"—she is brooding, alone, sits in the middle of the triangle of chair and table with head lowered in long widow's despair—she whose face last night I saw bending over my sleep with an expression of unfathomable meaning I know is love on earth—and who was ironing all my clothes while I had these tragic dreams—

BARBARA DALE AND HER HUSBAND at their new home in Lowell on the first floor of the Lilly-Hildreth house where I'd lived in my childhood of 6, Irwin and I go visit—same house, I am amazed, it's Christmas—from the yard B's husband (ostensibly Marlon Brando) calls down "Get some gin and water" but in trying to give us money I reassure we have it—and Irwin and I softly go to "Ralph's" store which is "still there" (25 years! on the corner) and old Canucks are sitting in there in vast families in brown gloom—I come in say, "Une douzaine d'eu... d'oeufs—" —remembering to pronounce it right, a dozen eggs, and the old Bowlegs cuts out into the back to get em and is gone a long time—meanwhile one of his daughters, as if because tho I'm polite and smiling I havent taken off my baseball hat reaches out and snaps my bra-strap thru my clothes, against my back, which doesnt perturb me—Earlier I'd been in some Obispo training Monastery with Book Rooms and Monk Head Coaches looking for me—impossible, not to be found, and hiding and cutting around yards, out to the Barbecue Fields—etc.—sheepish—Last night it was Joe laughing, leaning to tap me on knees, saying articulate Canuck joke, jumping up Hyah! hyah!

and putting on hat to leave—as of yore—but there are Two Joes and I'm glad one met the other (hints of Cody, or Somebody) and there's a spectral lunchroom in rainy Stony Boston Chicago of the Dreamglooms where Joe and I go—his car—the return of the old Joe of Salem street—

(incidentally B Dale and husband had a little niece who was playing a spinet piano behind a screen in the kitchen)

POP AND I ARE TRAVELING on some train in some bright land, the train takes a siding for some important scheduled Superior train and so for some reason big fat Pa follows me who in my own foolishness-follow-follow the "conductor" down some ramp to throw the switch so that as soon's the superior train passes (and it nothing but a Mail Car of Death self-operated, alone, gray, sinister) (cutting down the track silently) I help the conductor throw the switch (tie the, lock the Mainline Switch) and he and all other trainmen watching are laffing at me, tho Pop is serious, so that when it's done and climb out of the ramp up iron rungs of a ladder and see the rear car (smiling trainmen waiting) so give the Hiball Sign to show I know speed and need to go—'mid laffter I start running in snow and soft rockbeds to catch up to departing train and have a real hard time and have to sprint like trackster (as they cheer) (and somehow Pop and the Conductor are left behind anyhow)—running, knee pumping, kidwise proud to catch up to that observation car slipping away—blushing in winter, realizing they laugh, an old old feeling—Earlier the train was a bus and Pa was Ma—Ma and I were going somewhere, sitting in hard backseat and people left and I grabbed a soft seat reminiscent of the time I preferred soft window seats of Broadway Bus with Ma on Radio City day, to back seats hard and with motor hot—

AT A BIG "SWENSON" PARTY in his huge complicated hard-to-find-your-way-around apartments, there's been a weekend, drinking—We've gone down the street of some mixed-up California town (Los Altos!) and saw a colored girl across the street, wellknown, to whom one of our party called, "Come on over Joo Jee!"—and she derisively said no, with a remark, waving, going on alone, the colored guy in our party emphatically saying to me "You should know Joo Jee, you really should know her—she's something—" and later the big banquet for everybody—hysterical eaters—I start in the kitchen with tidbits on the table, toast butter and crisp in a dish on a side board, various crumbs en route in the livingroom, ending up in the parlor where people are standing or sitting around in various attitudes of wellfedness, not saying much, picking their teeth, drinking black coffee, or port, or Scotch—I see a lovely pecan pie in the middle of the diningroom table and take a knife to cut a piece, which brings it to the attention of everyone else so that when I wake up we've all slowly silently stepped up a tempo at the pie, cutting, lifting pieces, dropping them, hands mixing and clashing and sweating as at gold, hands trembling in growing hunger as the more Swenson morsels are laid out and the better, the hungrier more desperate the dark voracious guests fighting now to freeload at the curious pecan pie "I discovered"—but the whole dream filled with the gray indissoluble hopelessness like a stone —an emptybelly 3-beer nightmare, alcoholically lost, grim—

THEY'RE HANGING THE POLITICAL TRAITOR in my closet up in my room at Phebe Avenue, crowd watching from near the window and I (with friend) from near the corner—It's an old man like the actor Ray Collins, he isnt too scared, not at all in fact—The executioner puts the rope around his neck and for an instant we see a look of distaste (for the rope) (itself) (not Death) on the face of the condemned old man—I stand horrified to see it's all "really going to happen!"—the hangman ties the knot and then with no ado puts up laboriously the body of the big man, I had intended not to "watch" but I do "see" and the rope tightens, the politician grimaces to choke, his body rises, silent—no complaint—no comment from the audience—I "dream" his twisted side down deadneck, not moved at all but curious—going downstairs then with Lionel to the parlor where I turn on the television though it's 5 A M and Ma's in the kitchen cheerily making her go-to-work lunch and chatting with also up Nin—I say to Lionel "But he really wasnt all Anti Fascist!" and it's my father I'm talking about, my father was hanged—My mother looks at me as if she didnt recognize me immediately or what I was doing down there—The red livingroom rattle furniture of Lilly Street flat in 1929 is responsible for the horror, the hanging, the guilt, the old Victrola's just a new TV now, is all—the coffin that's never been removed from the parlor of the Kerouacs—le mort dans salle des Kerouac—

WILDERNESS OF VIRGINIA after awhile, the bus carrying me west to "Oakland" and on which I've been sleeping with head down on the top of the back rest ever since New York and so profoundly that some tall blond guy got on and sneaked into my window seat thinking himself in but I pretend to flop over and eventually he shifts to another seat—it's the distinct Virginia woods and the bus goes through a little town with Alpine like houses every one inn-like humming with excitement and voices of eaters, I think "They come in old country cars from down every hill, to the taverns of town"—As on my great voyage west in August 1952 across Carolina to the Coast, the sky is blood red in a rainy dusk, through trees far across the marsh I see the remnant red fire beneath a lowering night, outlining thin birch and stumps of America-lost trees—On the bus are two young railroad men one wearing a passenger cap, they're "deadheading" up the mountain to a train, some train order station in the bleak pines—I'm going to chat with them after my nap—In my dream-nap I imagine the bus is going thru Santa Margarita and with I was there, have nostalgia memories of Obispo and the little hill-swinger's shack at the trackside at Margarita so sweet and peaceful—America is so sad, haunted, long remembered, itself a dream, what can Irwin Swenson begin to know about the red dusks over the wilderness trees and the meaning of young trainmen in the hills, old shanties with stoves, the long old dream—Also I see visions of the war in Italy and see a truckload of American soldiers go by but in the Italian's naive picture of Americans they're all wailing together in one great bop band ensemble like Ted Heath or Neal Hefti band and I wake up realizing the Jazz Century I'm in and the thousands of dollars BEAT GENERATION which M.C.A. Agency lost, is worth—the big issues jazz will be, bop, and how Watson has already begun to capitalize on it at my expense (using my anecdotes, phrases etc. and in fact further battening on the sufferings of junkey musicians)—I feel horrified and fear my Blake humilities which I can stand will become unbearable if worth thousands to writers like Watson, as if and just like, Christ and his thorns pounded into a golden Chalice, the bible a Bestseller,—the Agony in the Garden a smash hit!

I'M EATING JUNE BEAUTY in a second story bedroom somewhere near the Bunker Hill Street of the White Horse Going East where the night before we'd been looking for secret dark places to ball, in the moonlight shadow of a house drawing up our open bed or vehicle but once started realizing it wasnt so dark and inside the house of the sad dim red windows maybe they see us (hints of Pauline Cole and I in the soft oral darkness laughing)—I'm not rich, not poor, happy in loves—Now we're in a daytime room and she's sitting on a stool like Irene's red iron stool and I'm kneeling wailing at her, she arches back with ecstasy, I chew & work—suddenly I realize a whole bunch of workmen at the nextdoor roof can see all but they every one pretend not to be looking at all by the time (passion spent, blindness done) I look up, we have giant double windows showing the whole roof—also across the alley a woman in this morning is laughing, vaguely in my sexing I'd thought it was because she saw us but I didnt care—Still, now, she laughs as I goop looking around for possible watcher suspects there in the room of eternity with my naked beauty—

THEY'RE HITTING FUNGOES in the Bridge St ball park fields of my boyhood in Centralville—it's "Coach Frank Leahy" and the kids (of 10, less, and up)—I'm in deep left scrambling after long fouls in the great weeds lost hidden rubbergreen Rousseau wildernesses where the blacktape balls roll—I make several lazy catches, dropping some—The point is, I want to work up to the plate and get my licks but the "game" is desultory and unorganized and I even sense it'll never last long enuf to get to me and anyway no one notices my presence in the outfield, I'm as inconspicuous, lost, and anonymous out there as a 7 year old ballchaser—So I go, into yards, around tennis courts, weeds, etc. retrieving—and finally game ends and so I'm later walking around in the 'school' hall located at Hildreth end of the field (where eternity red barn) and there's G.J. though he's also strangely Irwin (Mouse has become Irwin?) and I say sourly "Them Jews out there got me all chasin the ball then quit, the bastard Jews" and like Irwin

Mouse resents my sullenness and irrational cursing 'paranoiac' hostility to everything and goes off weary of me and I sense everyone else is also weary (like Lousy too) and I feel cold as a stone, abandoned, stupid, further irritated and incensed that now my own friends turn on me for a show of rages I always had and my father had, it's become "unfashionable" that's what—

A WHOLE BUNCH OF GUYS with me in some kind of Newport Bootcamp Barracks—I hear I've got $27 compensation waiting for me in the Commissary—we cut out to the cafeteria for sundaes, instead of my oldentime hot fudge I order strawberry with marshmallow—in the huge barrack sodaparlor shack the orders are repeated over a mike by a Chief Petty Officer—dumbwaiters carry iron rack trays up—Anxiously I picture in my mind the hurrying hurrying flurrying hands of the sundaemakers upstairs fluttering over our order of seven diverse sundaes—I watch the dumbwaiter, a tray-box is coming down—Irene and I comment and watch—but it's empty—only some little sad dumbkid comes down and then yells up the noisy wooden stairs and so still I picture the hurrying hands, the ice cream, the topping, the cherries, nuts, the swift work like at Jahn's—I picture it and <u>time</u> it in my anxiety to eat and so does Irene—meanwhile my companions are big careless joking Boots or Seadog Brutes who arent anxious for mere icecream—The center of the dream's interest is only once rememberable and therefore once really writeable and so from now on I'll remember the dream only at this dreambook pad because everything of tonight's dreams is lost, including a great awful sequence about a Beast, a Monster crawling—lost at the first official recall of the pillow—because in remembering and making mental note the brain is stiffened steadfast and no more opening (as of a bladder undulating) remains possible—merde!

$2.52 IS THE PRICE they're charging for the new French bilingual movie in the movie house across the street presumably on Avenue A—the boxoffice is across the street, the girl is telling me it's a "high class" audience—"You mean just well dressed" I scoff—Meanwhile her boyfriend tries to talk thru the little cage window hole—This is not the boxoffice but an information booth, though people are lined up and Irene is reading a paper and holding a woman's umbrella for her as she stands in line—Okay, we go to the boxoffice at the foyer and there's the awful price, this new picture has titles in French, Italian, English, German, the works—I catch a quick glimpse inside of a scene of a light-haired man gawping, the screen itself is unusually white—The old tickettaker woman who is the candy store owner old Jewess in Richmond, watched me with averted eyes lest I see too much (she's wearing slacks)—Five bucks is too much for a show, Irene and I cut

MARY PALMER earlier, on a bus trip "from Lowell to New York via Worcester-Springfield" with all Puerto Ricans living and traveling there now, Mary has a bunk and lays back reading and I see her after the halfway mark arrival at "Worcester" when with two Puerto Ricans I admired the setting sun on spectral redbrick American walls—I'm going to lie down with Mary, I cried "Mary!"—she doesnt mind, moves over, but her jealous redhead boyfriend glares at her and I cut out to back of bus for ordinary seat preferring darkness and solitude at window for remainder of trip to the River of New York—a man is dozing in the seat leaving the window open for me, I slip in

SOME AWFUL MANIAC is attacking me, keeps punching at my groin with iron fingers, gnashing teeth, I cant keep him away or understand him, no one helps me, I wake up with a belly ache—Earlier Mickey Mantle'd hit a homerun in the Stadium of Dreams, there where I was after our long drive (300 miles) from Maine to New York and suddenly in the gray luminosity there's all Lowell-Manhattan on its Merrimac-Hudson shining and the driver was terrific—Mary Palmer or somebody with me—and like driving back from Lawrence of Salisbury Beach in youngdays and Sunday afternoon there's redbrick Lowell still and the mills are quiet, the cartons outside canal warehouses sit in long shadow gloom beneath those eternity smokestacks—the Homerun by Mantle is a ball I myself catch caroming off other strugglers, but an attendant wants it back—it's way up in the "mile high balcony" where I've been before—It's later in a backroom after some events in a frontroom having to do with truancy the mad bastard starts wrestling with me, nameless horrors like being tickled but viciously, I remember crying out "If there's anything I cant stand is someone who is queer and insane at the same time."

I GO BACK TO MEXICO BUT HATE IT, I'm with Irene—take a long walk with her down on San Juan Letran in the daytime saying "I know these streets very well" and figure on taking her to lunch in an earlier dreamplace I'd seen with Dave Sherman, which now I cant find—Somehow too I'm alone and carrying a white seabag and as I see two, three guys in the street I remember the dream of having my seabag robbed and hurry on—There is a long sad dirty Fellaheen street, I took the wrong road trying to return to downtown, I tell this to some guy in a car who's backing up but he's too stupid to care altho he understands and doesnt offer me a lift—God the weariness, bleakness of my eternal mistake—I'm back in a, in _the_ Mexico of Unreality—with Irene I figure I'll live in this tenement but when she hangs up clothes everyone'll be staring at her especially the soldiers in the last windows, American soldiers—I have a small sad temporary room near the old dream Medellin-Roebuck of original 1950 Weed Afternoons—Earlier I'd been in California and planning to work railroad there "out of San Diego" and make it, there'd been a conductor—all, all unreal and dreams—the voyages in between—Finally, alone, I do have lunch in some place, with a bunch of men speaking good English, I make a mental note to bring baby there—it's funny food, little cactus plants in pots, wet—to get there we've had to tread lightly thru highly charged organic water two inches deep and warned not to splash or walk too deep—This is the food of the great sad dangerous water—cactus peotl like little plants hot and steamed, brussels sprouts small and pale green, and one dish I have which is told to me as being the greatest: a kind of eggplant-looking or boudin-looking (French hot blood sausage) skin—or like Jewish intestine skin, etc.—I eat a big dish of everything thinking "Well I finally found a place for lunch anyway tho I wonder if the 'water' business is not just a lure to get customers and these pleasant men just restaurateur hustleurs"—While lost in the side sand road I'd seen the skyline of the city lost and twisted in another direction like the time I lost the center of San Luis Obispo walking around the elongated mountain—Mexico Shmexico this is too much loneliness and loss

A KIND OF SHIP'S CREW OF MEN all together in a cafeteria group where they've been eating, about 50, 60—elegant people like Hubbard, W H Auden, many others, Swenson presumably—It's like the Lowell High School basement lunchroom so vast, dark—After I've been notified my time to work has come I go to the bar to eat, I'm sitting down with a group—Another pisses outdoors headed for the next bar, someone says "Why do they keep going to that other place?"—W H Auden comes in and for "the first time" is sitting next to me and I notice he may talk to me—I've just written something brilliant—We begin talking about some joke drink—"Woman's piss" we'll call it—"Only" I add (laughing) (heartily) "we'll call it by some other name—woman's urinary"—we search philologically—

OCT 14 '53—I'M BACK ON A SLEETY NIGHT on Moody Street or that is the street is covered with a film of white frost—I've been to Destouches' where people heartily laughed, then thought of writing the "wrinkly tar" corner of Dr Sax fame and thinking "I'll see Scotty and Lousy I wont be surprised"— Suddenly I see "Duke Gringas'" young brother come clomping, I see just his shadow in the melancholy dusk, he's been walking all the way from the Library with books underarm "like I used to do" and I think: "I'll ask him, hey Gringas! Hey! Where's your brother Duke, Menelaeus?—" I figure he's a big scholar, also was a football star, unmistakably a Gringas with his big clomp boot shoes fromming in the snow and his long Santoslike chin and Russian ears and gangly angle walk—I am very aware of the new generations of kids of Pawtucketville and look around, I'd just seen two others "like young brothers" of "so and so"—I head for Blezan's store conscious of the dream and determined to "make it come true" and the fine sleet white strengthens my belief in the unreality of the older "snow dream" of Moody but the thinner (more believable therefore) realities of this one—Kid Gringas in the sad dusk has that same sharp and humangrieving reality I saw in the "moonlight bum caps of Amsterdam" and many other dreams where figures stalk cleanly and sharp in soft gloom clouds of poor nap (H horror) brain

---

(real nights long ago when I'd go to Destouches for 7 caramels a penny and one had rocks and I'd chew that slowly over Operator 5 with the first one crossing the park, the familiar dust underfoot)

G J'S AT HOME in Lowell, at his mother's, has matured into a funny conversational intense loafer———sits in the kitchen all day with the boys, one of them is Georgie the Polock who's telling him his usual stock of funny fantastic and murderous stories (like the one about killing three cops in a Marseilles air raid) only G J doesnt believe a word and immediately makes fun of him "There he goes O O O what a liar!" and I see a great slur of hope in Georgie's green eyes, they glow pale phosphorescent green and he looks at me, slitting them as if to say "See? I've finally found a man who fills me with great interested joy because he knows I'm a liar and I'll never give in and admit to him"—"Ha!"—a great Polish Liar telling Tales and there's all the slobs of the Kitchen Sea believing in his bullshit tales but not hometown matured G J in his Eternity Middens there— What crazy buddies they make in all this laterlife dreambleak—There is faint rigging in the gloomy as-of-ships background—They are sitting face to face in old age chairs in the middle of the room—I think Scotcho may have been around earlier—

I dreamed of the park too, "the familiar dust underfoot" was a prophecy phrase of this dream, and there's murder or horror and death in it, corpses,—the dry cornfield,—a man, dead—adventures in the doom gloom,—Larry Charity—not Larry Charity but Kid Taki —I've forgotten-his-Name—the Gershom tenement blocks, the Omaha garage, Riverside Street and the Giant Iron Tree—the old Houses, the graveyards underneath, the Sunk Bleak of Lost

Which now in solitude
I dive into once more

in own silent room
of mind serene
remembering
the world

'IT'S SOMETHING HAPPENING BETWEEN ME AND POP, in Centralville—in the trellised rose sadness of the little cottage on West Street which had Christmas in its eyes long ago we are closer than ever, it's he returned from the dead and I'm grownup and thirty but we live in West St and have profound absorptions together as others watch interested—For some holy reason the entire thing is kept from my mind in details, I can only say "J'ai rêvez d Papa"—

EATING LUNCH IN THE POLICE STATION are Bull and I and Raphael or somebody,—Bull is drinking some of the new coffee substitute with a funny name like PREEN, it has no caffeine in it and looks just like coffee—as he stirs and takes his first sip I watch and wait—"Well?"—He makes a face, "No good"—I'd just been reading an article about how there is going to be Prohibition of smoking in America and very soon—in a loud gleeful voice I say "Just like in the Twenties when people went to Europe to get soused—they'll all start goin to North Africa and places to smoke—and you know what they'll smoke—haw haw haw!"—and in a loud voice but no one of the cops in the sideroom care or notice, they're in a dark room with wet film, in shirtsleeves—The scene slightly shifts as we're eating a big dinner now in a Mexico City cafeteria and my dessert is a little glass bowl of bread pudding on the sides burnt and sticking, at which I pick desultorily as we talk and Bull, getting up to carry plates back to the counter, without consulting me and maternally picks it up and carries it back as if he didnt want me to pick at remains like a vulture and get fat and I smile to think of it—Earlier we'd been standing around on the sidewalk... it's some foreign country or other—As I consider the fact of everyone giving up smoking further and further into hiding with my Opium Pipe—this is the 1% top part of a vast 99—Ag!

THE DIVEBOMB PILOT, he's way up in the sky ready to fall and open his chute,—it's me—I fall a long ways but aint scared and there's a long way to go judging from the landscape so when I do open my chute I feel I've made a mistake and will spend all afternoon floating down to earth —I've my cat in my arms—

Later down on earth I'm working among boxcars and sheds with a bunch, "in the South," one fellow paints two boxcars dazzling silver and one blinding gold, so bright you cant look at them in the sun—the fellow is big Ted Joyner of the South redfaced and puttery with brushes——"How can we work those cars now!" I think pettishly—Other events—around Easonburg Crossroads—Ma—

BIG FIRE HAD DESTROYED whole blocks in New York so they're excavating and filled in cement foundations and now are driving holes down in for foundation rods and I'm trapped on the high slipping bank of sand and rocks trying to get behind the fence but afraid it's too rickety and unsafe to grab—very high up to look down—An old foreman comes along and tells me it's safe to catch the fence—He keeps feeling my ass, inspecting my blue railroad handkerchief presumably for come—Earlier I'd made an appointment to meet Uncle Mike in the railroad station, the Pennsylvania, at the information booth,—we're going to Nashua together—I know I'll cry all the way all the time and he too—There he is in a far corner of the station waving at me as if bashfully and uncertain he's waving to the right person—I'm at a train door, he's in a ticket corner, neither one of us in the right meet-spot—I go on over—This was arranged during a big weekend at Aunt Clementine's house which was just like the one at 'Fortier's' last night when I slept on the double bed with Donnie—Sitting in the kitchen all the relatives—Poor sad Mononcle Mike with his black umbrella how I wish I'd have known him in my maturity—what stain of sorrow is't fills a grave in Nashua now—along side the other vast stain of sad spot of Pop—and the little inheriting one, Gerard—

BIG FLAMING AIRPLANES TRYING TO LAND in the New York-New Jersey airport in broad daylight disaster two of them are floundering across the sky to crash in the meadows of junk—I'm watching from the field after a bus trip from somewhere North where I had a suitcase and a bag of big marbles (big bag) and stored them in the bus compartment myself in an attempt to save the marbles (for Lil Luke) after I'd goofed and taken a walk down the bus hiway city then saw I had to get back as soon as possible and only way to be on time was cab, more expensive than the bus trip itself!—so hurried—and now in field the DC-6's falling in orange sweptback flame—Later according to instructions contained in the Almanac of Mystery and mark't on the Map of Bayonne I go to Bayonne to the Ottoman Temple older than America made of wood Byzantium in splintered gray cracks, so old, like the barges at Communipaw waters—I sneak around on dangerous boards looking for the altar, I can see all big glittering New York across the river—it ends up I'm inside naked with little Philip and someone else presumably my young sister and we're all naked, I'm trying to take my choice but at same time I'm concerned (because pale and infantile) with other things, like airplanes and meaning of Temples—It was an Arabic Pseudomorphic overlay on the rusts of Jersey that no historian'd yet noticed and it was so strange, it has to do with those knives and Burma caves of horror, something's deep inside, rituals of Snake and Old Sanskrit Secrets—Who was That He Man who wanted to fight me? I sure was ready for im

I'M GOING TO DRAW A BIG PICTURE FOR THE NAVY of the Rock Island streamline train coming into the Frisco City on a trestle over the blue water and a ship coming in beside it, one half of the left page of the big 2-page spread color-drawing will show the towers of the city, then the Diesel pulling only a few coaches, then the water traffic —anyway, I'm on a pier to do this and at one point just sit around waiting like at Merrimack Square the shoeshine of Five-and-Ten Back Corner but on the wood warp drowse afternoon of slap gulls with Nin sit and talk, something Navified, on duty, waiting, and also reminiscent of parts of the Boott Millyards, the loading ramps—Earlier and probably connected I'd been in the showers with all the Marines, I see myself there fat, I refuse to fight with any of the Marines especially the red haired one ("they have knife tricks")—The 'sketching' having to do too with earlier, also in Navy or Marines, Robert Whitmore my buddy of the S. S. Carruth is showing me how he describes an apartment building when he writes, "the wander wada rada rall a gonna gay, Zack!" the flow of words and the releasing bop-sound at the end of a prose rhythm paragraph—we're laughing like hell—there'd been great events enroute and in and out of the barracks which at one point melted into Joe Fortier's big Bridge Street house and the great dream of Doctor Sax's haunted house

DOCTOR SAX'S HAUNTED HOUSE—it's night, I'm with Bertha and Phillip at the Fortier house, there are lights in the (now occupied and not wrecked haunted) house on the hill way up the other side of the street—I see the shadow of a pacing figure in the fireplace flickers golden livingroom, huge—lights in many windows—"Wow!"I say "Doctor Sax the actual now real flesh Doctor Sax or heir apparent to that mad title of my Lowell Dream is stalking up and down the parlor with the cocktail like mad Hubbard at cocktail hour or some frantic James Mason Lord"—the night, the gold light in some of the windows of the manse showing thru the thick pines of the bigslope lawn that rises from the sidewalk stonewall on Bridge Street—"Come on Phillip let's sneak up the grass and investigate"—We sneak across the street, in the moonlight, lo, there's a cut of old sad boxcars in the spur on Bridge Street, one of them's on our way so I push it, 'kick it' somehow and it rolls into the lawn-track of the haunted house and so fast and far I'm worried it's going to hit the deadend block or go over the spur mound and derail or even bounce back and roll back on us so with keen eye fixed on the floom of mist moon ahead I wait awhile before starting with Phillip shh to wiggle up the lawn—Now we're crawling, we come to a mound, under a pine, suddenly there's the proprietor Mad Sax himself stalking in the blind moonlight grass with rifle and revolver, we flatten and watch—Somehow he's walking straight for us by mistake and suddenly he's even walking over the mound and coming down right on us and that's when I see the sheriff's Badge he's wearing and he's gonna step over us accidentally or sinisterly knowing anyway so I jump up and shout—the Mad Sax Sheriff begins yelling "Bang! Bang!" the guns are just toys but he's very annoying and keeps pushing me back and laughing or yarking savagely with maniacal Hyde-like intensity and I jump back in horror, he doesnt molest Phillip, there's another "sheriff" nearby to whom I plan to appeal for aid as I jump and dance back in the now gray afternoon grass before the thrusts and bang bangs of the teethshowing old maniac with toy guns and badge who's sore cause we wanted to sneak up and watch him pace in his Eternity Mansion at Cocktail Fireplace Hour—shouting and cackling at me like that maniac tickling me last week—

A LONG BICYCLE RACE TO LAWRENCE which I win—there's also a stretch where you run and pick up your bicycle off the sand road, which I rode swooping on the banks like a motorcycle champion in a carnival pit—the forlornness of those piney barrens, that sand road, of the puffing lone racer!—I win the race and come back to the big house on Salem Street where June and Ma (reconciled) are waiting for me, June is at the gate, beautiful, we whisper promises of the night to each other—her body is firm, warm, her breast spots stick me delightfully, she's as white and openable as that veritable Oyster Girl —in the house she's in the davenport sunporch sewing, Ma's in the kitchen with arrays of pans and pots in a partitioned section in the middle of a huge kitchen—Later June and I are shipping out, thru some friends of mine "because I'm too crazy or too wild or too something to be a deckhand" I'm going to be made Steward, Chief, and there sit June & I in the Officers' Mess eating with the Engineer Department Officers—at one point the 3rd Assistant says "But no milk"—"I'll get you milk!" I say "after all if I'm gonna be Steward"—the ship's still in port, I run down to the stores and search frantically in dark lockers and funny little big-covered-but-small-insided iceboxes horizontally shaped (to the deck)—finally in a horrible burlap canvas bag prop icebox like the horror bag of the Kafka nightmare hero dragging his dragon green be-buttoned caterpillar machine burden bag across the gray strange stage of eternity racks and dust, I find plenty of milk and also new socks and all kinds of mixed up stores (I'd just in a wooden icebox rejected half empty milk containers)—here I find brand new ones (because I'd thought I'd detected sour milk scabs thru the transparent paraffin cover)—here's all new milk and I start to leave but the burlap bag has wrapped itself and almost grown tightly around my waist while I rummaged and all by design, it's a Trap Icebox of the Ship to catch culprits and have them wander forlornly on the bridge with the big bag dragging around them like a robe of shame but a great "holding the bag" or "draggin the bag" super horror Shame—I tug, it's tight around me, insistent, I'm trapped —Earlier it had been great singing of the Rigoletto Company, gladness, I was there with them—and the words: "Cad Pa L.I. Canada"—

(O that back-around-me sneaking strait-jacket!)

"HER MILKY ENGINE BEGINS" is the sexy saying about the Ava Gardner beauty in the story—the Enguardiente Indians, "original inhabitors of California" and therefore obviously Pomo group of fierce organized fighters are going to raid a fort in 1850, we see their naked forms sneaking along the roof, it's explained how they set fire to the fort by placing dry bramble bundles under foundation posts—We also see the boiler rooms they're afraid to go into, the underground damp room where I thought of living but changed my mind—No white men about—We see the great Enguardientes practising on a pale green hill, cavalry charges on horseback, volleys of fusiliers riddling targets in one fire so you see the big balloons explode in popping smokes—Earlier we'd all been afraid of the atom bomb hitting over the Merrimac River and in fact, I'd "daydreamed" it or it otherwise happened, dark gloom over all our souls as we wait hidden and huddled on Lakeview Street (facing from where I was born)—disaster and Armageddon in the Dark Air of my birth, over the river of life—

After the great tragedy of "Camille" the young priests begin playing touch football with the visiting Scandinavian champions in the street—they're sensational —a great gang of nuns passes, en route to the pastry shop for coffee—the game is sensational, long passes, long runs, fingertip catches, cries, trolleys passing, it's a great <u>comedy</u>, and is the last part of the tragedy of Camille—I'm watching with Nin—it's like Liverpool Merseyside—

IN THE PACIFIC ON AN N. M. U. SHIP, as pantryman at first and with a galley crew of 50 to wash dishes for, a cargo passenger ship, I got the job so fast I'm amazed and there I am in apron at the greasy sink among the yelling golden guys and staggering with dishes down the grey alleyway to the strange little pantry where I rack em up—and the ship is two days outbound for the Orient—nevertheless in some spectral cove another ship pulls alongside and I go out thru the porthole and return to America ending up childlike gooking at the window of home on Gershom Avenue in Lowell in broad afternoon with a sheet a shroud or blanket over my head looking out on the street thru the gray dim cloth—looking out on the big tenement and there's a Negro workman staring at me from his ledge trying to figure out what I am—it's the old useless hanging around the house not-working sick neurotic ship-jumping school hookeying Ti Jean trying to find his lost brother in the parlor glooms—At the end I see the beginning of the movie Two Years Before the Mast with the same two old guys embracing in surprise in a trellised sea garden—

IN WATSONVILLE CALIFORNIA with my mother suddenly (in the marshes outside, at around Elkhorn or Moss Landing that Steinbeck wrote about and where I braked on the SP) we see a flock of flying snakes, reminiscent too of those seahorses in the picture yesterday and green and with little curved-for-flying spine bodies and the faint suggestion of transparent butterfly whirrers and awfully disgusting—"C'est des cockrelles," my mother says with great disdain and disgust, "They're just cockroaches"—she's not fooled—they're cockroach people impersonating as flying snakes and she's seen it before—At once I'm reminded of Irwin Garden (Pa called him cockroach), Hubbard, all my friends my mother hates & fears and in fact one of the snakes suddenly flops over my neck "like Garden!" I think frantically dodging to run, "like the importunate advances of affection from my disgusting friends!"—the flock of snakes over the marsh fly away—

Later, right after, I see a vision of the Katzenjammer kid that had dark hair, striped shirt, he's pulling down a prize box from heaven on a rope and pulley, it turns out to be a mother with gifts—

PA AND I BLEARILY on the seats of some passenger train sit talking about his illness and what they've been saying to him down at the Union, about which he is very vague—He's going to die just enough if he hasnt already—Ma and I discuss it—God how heavily he carries his carrion corpse around in these repetitious dreams, with what a hopeless, pale, almost invisible face, so joyless; so far gone from all hopes of the living and even from the bleak recognition of the bitchness of existence (which doesnt bother him any more he's so listless) (in fact returned from the grave)—This is our sweet Papa of starry night pasts when we grow up and grow old in this world the least of which you can say is that it leaves a bad taste in your mouth, like iron—Jawbleak gumming irons of no-hope morns, shit on the branch of peace—There was another, special high rack where I was hysterical—This was all dreamed last night and gone now memory-wise—Night before I'd returned to Nin's house in Carolina, Luke driving me up in the puddly driveway and Nin far from greeting me gayly asks first I help her with the suitcase then when she does talk it's but coldly and asking why I came and why dont I straighten out—bleak little wood white cottage in the open flats on the highway, dreamed and seen before, and big gray grass wintermud yard—and Big Luke makes no comment, Lil Luke dont care—there's also a dog—

A HENRY FONDA MOVIE about pirates at sea, but he's impersonating some kind of woman and we see him hysterically packing to leave the ship and pulling things out of his closet including such beautiful flowing silken scarfs some of them blue as night we hear women in the audience say "Oh he's been stealing just the same"—and at the end the movie (strange enuf already) no makeup and you see him go down the outside stairs plain faced, graystark, and you know the movie will again take a piratical romantic turn when the real Henry returns from the pirate ship captaincy with makeup and well combed and will be standing straight, handsome and indignant in the middle of the girl's room denouncing the other Henry—the people who are putting on this movie over TV are already getting letters from viewers in Greenwich Village saying they never knew about this great picture and it's old, 15, 12 years old—they want to know the names of all the cast—an old undertrodden neglected film masterpiece of Henry Fonda's early past

OVER THE GIANT JUNK FLATS OF AIKEN STREET and Laurier Park and Hoboken New Jersey of plane crashes and rust, in bright sunny day, I watch airplanes fly off and studied the stories of the pilots—then I go and find a dank vast hidden underpart of a Spectral World Barn or Dance-hall and go in there with a child like my mother or Phillip Fortier and crawl over a big oval rock to find hidden lumber and carpenter tools against the dripping well which has a bulb—Now I want to create a mystery fantasy in this rubbish cellar and suddenly begin to hear a heavy slow thumping—"The beating of a giant heart—A monster is hidden here!—They're building structures for it!"—Far off in the gloom plastered against the Great Wall of the Cellar I see the Giant World Crab but aint sure it's really just that or shadow, or something else more awful, more under may be heartbeating—it isnt real, I want to make the Monster Crab exists to write the story—I see families adventuring in the rubble

WAR—HORRIBLE INFANTRY WAR that made me wake up in the night and want to take off for the woods like Thoreau—I'm alone in a kind of schoolhouse surrounded on all sides by the Orientals who are firing from 100 yards across the fields and from the woods in back, burp guns, rifles, a constant racket and all aimed at me who am so innocent and childlike in the dream all I have is a goddam "pow" voice-gun to shoot with out of windows and even when windowpanes crash and enemy points big guns in at me to invade I aim the toy gun, "brow!"—I keep imagining the rain of bullets entering my body, the pain, but it doesnt yet happen—yet so many bullets are being fired at the little schoolhouse which is part Bartlett Jr Hi but only firstfloor and like the Haunted House across Joe's and something earlier, stranger,—so many bullets I couldnt help being hit—Finally it's a moonlight dawn and I have no real knowledge of how to get out of this predicament because suddenly I've found some real bullets and a real gun and I'm jammed a cartridge in but cant find the firing safety pin and an enemy pokes his gun in the window to kill me and all I do is raise the real gun and say pow—I had hopes of sneaking off thru the dark but in the moonlight whitening to dawn I can clearly see sneaking figures like Indians closing in—and couldnt make it thru them and out to safety, oblivion, beyond the wood—I wake up realizing I wish I were dead and thinking of the next war, I wont be able to live thru it, and thinking of the American soldiers in Korea bound hands-in-back bayoneted on the ground to real non-pow bleak winter frost death and blah I dont see why the West should suffer itself the indignity of living on the same globe with those Mongolian Idiots of the East, who came charging in suicide thousands in moonlight attacks and loved it—Pearl Harbor's just the beginning—They've given Attila battleships—I think there are supposed to be others dead, with me in the classroom—I dont see them or notice them in the strange general goldenness of the color of this horror and final despair dream—

I'M IN A CARIBBEAN COUNTRY racing over the water of the bay on a little boat which I push my feet out on and the harder and further I stretch it the faster it skims over the water—there are other boats, I'm a tourist—I come and bounce right on shore and go on skimming thru the streets and on the beach but noticing that the straw bottom is wearoutable—I walk in the narrow picturesque streets of the Carib village, wanting a woman—I see a strangely interesting looking but diseased-faced and old woman on a balcony and give her the eye, at first she pretends not to respond but then comes down after me—We go thru silent mysterious streets like in Victoria Mexico and the woman of the Fellaheen Hilltop Guitar—I am pleased that a man can always get laid in a Latin American country—

We get on the main street of the Village which is like the "San Obispo" Main Street that always runs into the town in exactly that manner—hilly, eventful—it changes to where Julien and I and presumably Irwin (or Bull) have been vacationing in this town and had our car parked in front of the Monastery Institution or Charity School, in front of the salmon wall—but the Headmaster is frowning in the wall gate saying we cant park there but I find a semihidden sign proving we can, and Julien's not too concerned and's working with luggage and cursing—

Since we're leaving this land I wind up in "Russell Jurgin's" or "GeneDexter's" or "Charley Williams" apartment gathering our belongings which got mixed there, the owner is out—I steal paper clips, look for useless stationery materials but deliberately leave unwanted shirts, socks (the purple ones), suspected pants (are they mine or his? the trip's been long) and I leave a valuable threesome of pictures one depicting Julien Love as Christ Crucified tearing and straining off the Cross but nailed tight so in a gigantic agony pose hanging golden and <u>mustached</u> from the wall of a cathedral and the reason the picture is so "valuable to Garden" is we see his large penis balling up in a loincloth and as viewed from below very erotic—this picture is captioned "By Elmont High School gang, 19—" and is marked J. Kerouac under to show who drew it. . . a great thing and I leave it for the occupant's concern—(showing spirituality of his rapacious-seeming visitors)—Rummaging in junk and pants and books all over parlor trying to take final things with me to final ends of the world—Ending up in a mess of hipsters and Dick Beck and going from one pad to another to connect and pick up green and a mixup of Television sets and I end up at Ma's house on Phebe Avenue, it's

Xmas, she steps on the couch, sleeps, I unplug the tiny hand portable TV in the sideroom and take it to the parlor to face her couch but am accidentally plugging up (carrying) the electric stand clock instead—I'm in my pajamas, the house is littered with stuff (the stand clock is covered with expensive leather)—and all started from an innocent joyride on a lake—(Shape of the foot boat was like a paper sailer you throw to ceiling—it sure went)

IN THE MIDDLE OF ZAZA GABOR'S DREARY gray afternoon tea which is going on somewhere else in the big sad house at the foot of Boisvert Street location of the old St. Louis de France nun's house where Nin had her sad bleak piano lessons on long red afternoons in New England winter and I played in the field of the Devils with my crunch boots—I'm in the toilet hiding and taking a crap and another guy a well dressed witty socialite like Kyle Elgins but dreary comes in or's already in and disturbs me in my revery—I'm trying to hide from the Russian Novel chatter of the ladies in that Gray Lace Breakable Livingroom and I imagine the dismalness of it as a little kid considering his aunts hordes of em—At some other point in the farce and force of unsleepy dreaming I learn that Zaza or the socialite man is sick and been ordered by the doctor to drive every day to New Jersey and eat pure cream ice cream, quarts of it and immediately I wanta go along or get some too, be sick too—Had a chance to get up at 8:30 and slept till Noon instead, for fear of what to do with all that morning—

VAGUELY IN A SICK DREAM a bunch of us guys are in an open space surrounded by watching crowds, a giant act of teamship and fellow-suffering duty is being enacted as each of us (tho casually and in the midst of continuing almost gay conversations) takes his turn in the center to receive the downward huge tho soft enough shock of some parachute of the sky, some battering ram of mentality and guilt but real, material, so as I take my turn just at the last second someone of my buddies saying "Jack Jack" I stand there and down it comes, white, big, flappy, and shivers my skull a moment in cottony recognition and frizzles my dream and having done its appointed slow ram of Eternity it rises up, bounces up high and far again, to almost out of sight, where it begins again the descent to earth (which it must never touch), where WE'LL be to receive it on our sacrificial skulls—Watchers say nothing, we talk and pass the time and even the stick, laughing, comradely, crazy together like a troupe of hot rod racers in heaven—

AL BINGHAM IS IN PRISON, but is a trusty and allowed to wander around in a prison suit or pajamas with number during the day—I visit him, we're climbing the steps to the iron cells and the area of the greensward yard hall—"Ugh" I say seeing iron gray bars as we come up gloomy steps together—He laughs radiantly and serenely—"That's just what Wallington said last week when he saw them—" Al is resigned, Buddhistic, not Christlike, like a Genêt hero quietly and hardly ironically enjoying jail, no complaints to make, or excuses, as tho he couldnt help being in prison but he could cease tormenting his mind even here—so I see his radiance and wonder at him—we come to the Yard Hall where all the other prisoners and their visitors are gathered some sitting on the slopey sward, some wandering around as in a Ginsbergian garden of Dolls, tender prisoners somehow, all in gray suits as 'trusties' and Bingham the kindest, most beautiful radiant of them and saintlike—all of it is so beautiful I find myself wishing I was in this kind prison—

THAT WILD CHICAGO-LIKE NEW YORK or 'rainy Pittsburgh' of Book of Dreams' first page—I'm stepping out from my 450 W 20 pad to eat a snack in a Bowery Brown Cafeteria like in the old Henry Street Vision of Joe when he and I among doleful garbage cans and amid plasters of city ruins walked, a dream as old as Russia with Joe stee-riding along purple popped to 'bout laugh 'Hyoo hyoo!' boots and all and in that Murder Garden gloom—now 'tis the other side of town but the same Bowery like darkness and after eating which takes me two hours and my thoughts so vast while eating that when I wake up and realize my mind'd run thru two hundred dreary mind-weary Finnegangs Wakes, half awake goofball sleep—somethin to do with a waitress girl, burns—I leave and head back home, to "First Avenue" tho geographically it's Eleventh Avenue West Side—going down bleak Boston-like black cobbles like the cobbles seen earlier in an afternoon redsun dream of Sheridan Square, Danny Richman and Bev Watson, I spy four colored girls rowdily walking under a lamp (like the lamps of the 59th Street New York small colonial Greekhouse Armistice celebration dream) (which I go to see Jack Anderson mysterious)—As I start trailing after them for sexual interest I notice four white girls following them rowdily but all with short haircuts and pants and Dikes—I follow—there are other prowling Greeks like me (in the pristine red city morning New York of brownbrick the Greeks of Sex)—it's like Boston and backa the Boott Mills—suddenly I realize I'll have to cut thru a restaurant to get to my street and back to my furnished room—I go thru a bustling golden cafeteria where a man rushes up to me and says a story about some blonde waitress somewhere who was so sloppy her sores ran while she served you—"Pimples," he said—I exhibit polite response but blankly he rushes off, so had I just stared at him gravely as I really wanted he would have persisted with something else (O the grief of the Lowell bridge over the canal, the old glassbroken walk for lovers on the canal lock wall, the nights I've jumped down dere per dream and in real life as a real boy prowled with Dicky and Who Else and the dream of the Flood Oersurmounting it) (with raging whitesmash, river mouth grashin to show clash crash)—drash!—brash!—Aoooowayyy br—a—a—shh—I move on thru the kitchen and out the back with instructions from Porto Rican scullions Late from the Chico Sea—I start up a flight of circular iron steps like the steps of Waterworks & City Clocks with fat Wipers in undershirts by valves reading the Union City Journal—I go another flight, contemplate a third, at each level the iron door is locked, I keep thinking one will be on some level unlocked and I'll be able from the outside to descend to my alley—but no door iron unlocked, the higher I go the more futile my search for homeward—I'm trapped in the steel & maniacal contrivance of the city—gotta go down again, start from the rear—Find some way to unlock the levels of my mind & get on in—woke up in iron red dawn of workday (at Post Office Mails) thinking: "I dont wanta go to no California & at red tired dawn my engine's waiting pointed to Watsonville three hours away—"

GABBING AS USUAL, in the Lowell City Hall Square with presumably Cody I've failed to notice the reason for Lil Timmy's big trip in the car, he grownup, 5, dressed in lil blue suit, Evelyn his Ma's been primping him & priming him for the big day as I gab, so it isnt until the last minute when they're getting in the car that I glance at their plan-itinerary & realize as on belatedly-guilt Tea seeing "Religion" & names of places in the booklet that I realize Lil Timmy's about to (and Gaby too) be <u>Confirmed</u> in a sense, big day, etc., O god I bore even myself with useless detail—failed to notice the kid's big day in the car driving to religious in new blue suit, because high gabbing in City Hall so see Evelyn aint interested in anything but her kids, as proper, and I wake up saying "Aint no sense my going bothering out there," that is, interrupting their lil serenities gabbing about myself—lil serenities of young parents and new children and all the calmities & lil joys of of the dust—For me it's immortality in a hut—

IN THE PARAMOUNT THEATER G.J. and Scotty and I are watching the ballet of the Black Men, sorta Negroes or Polynesians, muscular & graceful, reminding one again of the "Indian baggageman buddy of San Jose" (actually a big Frisco Portugese)—the muscles hard, shoulders round, thin, tight veins, the dances un-effeminate but manly & beautiful, up on the stage—It's that spectral Paramount Theater I'd taken Ma & Nin that night of Irene's 'candy job'—Going backstage & into areas of circular stairs just like back-restaurant of yesterday with G.J. and Scotty now I say "Let's have coffee, let's meet, where will you be?"—"How about the Ritz cafeteria?" I interrupt G.J. who's trying to say "X" cafeteria which is actually the right name and I know it but persist, saying, "Well it's the Ritz Hotel over it," really it's the spectral Astor—astral astor—so G.J. and Scotty nod, they seem (as in Lowell Middlesex sad return saloon dreams) to be unsure about me and as if looking at each other oddly—"In a half hour" I 'suggest'—really hanging them & cutting out before they can say no—cutting out in elevator to go backstage to borrow money for coffee & donuts, if I fail in loan G.J. & Scotty will have to pay mine—It's the backstage of Backstages, and since Repetitious Paragon Paramount is also that Hugeroom House of Eternity and stage of great confusions & racking dusts & events commending itself to the activity of the whole world—Later I'm a successful smiling New York Damon

Runyon young genius writer (like the me of 1949) in Central Park with my welldressed hatted friends all smiling, chatting, saying "Well where do we go now, what do?"—like Lionel, cronies of latenight cafeterias, of talks & sweetfaced well walletted well-relaxed Megalopolitan eagerness the only kind I might ever feature again if I ever come back (because of $)—to city for further sojourns—It's midafternoon winter and we're all idle in the park & only slightly dissolute (of responsibility souls) and goodlooking, like a team of scenarists goofing—like a bunch of Sigmund Rombergs—I fear G.J. & Scotty were never there to meet me—

A BUG CRAWLING OVER A ROUND BARREL like in the dream, eating 'peach meat' I think, as it crawls along, and it is a person—this in deepest sleep woke up by the cat, proving the greatest deepest dreams are unrecoverable to the ordinary morning-waking brain—The bug was probably me, and so deeply involved in nutriment I didnt think it strange—Later it was a long happy dream of the backyard in Phebe Avenue and Jack Elliot the Singin Cowboy has made a record which is selling a million copies & we're all together in the happy yard, a new house there, at one point there are three thin mattresses on the floor of a cold hut & happily I pick mine out (narrower but thicker) leaving no other choice to the other two guys, Jack & Someone—All forgotten by now, afternoon, saved so I could write "more completely" and this is the sad result.

My mind, the Mind, is too Vast to keep up with.

The bug was eating peach colored pumpkin like meat that was very familiar in the dream & therefore in some future world is already familiar—

SEX DREAM—Marie Fitzpatrick or somebody, and I, hot, go down the cellar stairs holding each others' organs—I have hers, she mine, as we descend steps slowly—We're gonna look for a place to work—It's the basement of the Fortier Hugehouse on Salem—I pick a little sidecellar coal room, gray with ashes, dank, and stand her against the wall as we wake up—Just sweet immediate wanting—she's slicking up breath in her hiss hot teeth—I'm grinding my molars in bighard girlholding grash—r-r-o-p!—We're gonna find a place to gnash our hot and juicy parts pole into hole in some hideout craphole of the great cellar, no one'll know, we'll have bare thighs and write on chalk on the wall and smack goosy flesh and have hot jumping juices in the ecstatic secret liplicking lollswallowing lip-lolling suckcellar hole, droop—I'll grab her bare rumps and squeeze and dump in, standing, the straight pole, up her roamous slit, deep, she'll part warm breath to huff—I'll grang her—spew spill flood her inside belly womb—flutter my knees—tickle her top—accidently plop in, God.

THE HATEFUL SHIP IN THE HATEFUL MISSISSIPPI, I'm late returning to it and finally on top of that it's not the right ship and I stumble around the early dawn deck —my bunk in the messmen foc'sle—after sad bad events in presumably New Orleans, drunkenness—my own real ship's gone upriver—

HAPPY DREAM OF CANADA, the illuminated Northern land—I'm there at first on Ste. Catherine or some other Boulevard with a bunch of brother French-Canadians and among old relatives and at one point Nat King Cole is there talking with my mother (is not dark, but light, friendly, I call him 'Nat')—We all go to the Harsh Northern School and are sitting (like the gray wood room of Mechanical Drawing class in Bartlett J H shack) and the teacher is a freckled redhaired Scotchman and acts a little contemptuous of the Frenchies, has his favorite teacher's boy in the front row and he too is a sarcastic freckled redhaired British Canadian—I've been close and talkative and like Saintly Ti Jean with everyone so now contemplatively I lean forward and study the situation, watch the teacher and his asskissing sarcastic prototype, and softly, in French, nodding, for I see it all and only because an outsider American Genius Canuck can see, "Ca-na-da"—(I say) Ca-na-daw—and my brother darkhaired anxious angry Canucks vehemently agree with me—"It's always them!" they cry and I see that sarcastic non-French smirk on the redheads' faces, smashable faces, something hateful I must have seen on Ste. Catherine St. in 1953 March, that arrogant Britishified look—or from ancestors' memories of old French-Indian canoe wars—Had I gone back to Canada I wouldnt have taken shit one from any non Frenchman of Canada...took everything from Brother Noel and mourned—but God the fist mashed face of my redhaired English Canadian enemy—

This was such a happy dream, I woke up at 5 AM from the comradeship and glow of it—no anger (as now, afternoon) at all—I should have written it at dawn—it was Ti Jean the happy Saint back among his loyal brothers at last—That's why

OLD SHIFTS TO ENTERTAIN OURSELVES, G.J. and Lousy and Scotty and I in adolescent immortal years, but in New York, that part of it (Thompson St) where GJ & Scot & I strolled that Sunday afternoon in 1940 when they visited big Columbia Zagg at Hartley Hall and we walked... long red sun on the cobbles of lower Manhattan, we walked among the haunted buildings of Wolfe and blue architect-light windows of below Canal office and engineering and factory buildings, we saw pushcarts of Bleecker and down to Skippy's boyhood Vesey but innocent of NY then—ending we took pictures on the steps of Avery Hall, stepping smartly with pipe, full of Walgreen Times Square sundaes and movies—the last diligent jokes of GJ with Scotty and the dice in the dorms, the last sad beer in Lions Den ere they jaloppied back to what they thought were their 'gloomy fates' back in Lowell—O what a great book I must now write about my entire life!—that lower New York of that 1940 walk, only now it's night, a bar, the influx of Porto Ricans in NY so great that the bar is full of PR girls dancing alone in the crowded jukebox floor, as we file doorward from the back room (as Pioneer Club) (Boys) the girls ogle and wiggle and I push thru the first one, (leading Zagg) trying to ignore them to the instructions of Buddha—they are scraggly Fellaheen brunettes—there are men sitting around laughing, it's the real present downtown Lower Village NY of actual gay Porto Ricans—I therefore lapse into thoughts and see Lousy, GJ & Scotty latching each to a girl and devise a beautiful sad French movie of love picturing them next day, each separately with his girl in a room, the serious tragic lover to be pimple-jawed Scotty surling and actually in love...comic relief Lousy and his funny girl...also GJ and his outrageous behavior and wild girl..."I'll keep myself out of this book," I think seriously, "it'll be better"—I picture the actual girls—

AN MG CAR or gametoy truck that I'm zooming across sunny plazas of Lowell on, by the City Hall, at first in almost (oldtime dream) Frisco like sunny bottom-of-hill plaza (that original vision of Van Ness or Fillmore hill as old as original visions of Deni Bleu in Marin City)—my speedy machine takes me around and I look up at the fading sun and see it has a few bloated stars as big as little suns near it and they're big (and round as globes) because bloating and waxing like moons at wane of day or at fade fall 'pon horizons—So I look and see the small swimming roes of fire in the fields of the globular moonstar and I'm terrified in that old Lowell dream of starry disaster... looking thru a glass as I ride swiftly in the machine I watch & ponder—realizing the star is huge for some recent reason but also just for wane-horizon reasons and the sun is faded, vague, orange—we come to an old house like the Ottoman Empire of Hackensack but across the street from Lowell Public Library and there I get off the car and wander around in further events with somebody, a distinct sensation of that music store nearby—I watch the seething pellets in the globe world-star, like orange spirochete

THE LANDLORD AND HIS ASSISTANT come to the Textile Lunch tenement where Ma and I've moved, we're living on the 2nd floor instead of 4th so that watching from Iddyboy's Gershom house which we've also occupied I measure the space between passing man's derby hat and the windows of our flat in the tenement and it leaves fewer inches than you'd expect, so we're not high at all—I'm in the kitchen alone, loafing, the landlord canuck and his younger assistant have just finished some repairing and are leaving me a paper that I'm to deliver downtown to the Rent Loan Bank not far from the music store—they begin dreary Lowellstreet instructions—for the prodigal returner—I experience momentary despair and bleakness of being back and subject to 'laws of Lowell' again, so long desdone out of—The assistant is a definite snickering little curious Pawtucketville kid I'm bound to see that night in the Social Club alleys with Gene Plouffe and all the others and it's going to be just like Ste. Catherine Street saloons, beer, smoke, talk, bleak wintry city streets of Lowell Canada—not a happy or even interesting dream—So I was loath to even write it, and the sun star, and am doing it out of a sense of duty existence of which is reasonless at this late stage in my search for repose beyond fate and rest beyond heaven

WRITING DREAMS, TAKE NOTE OF THE WAY THE DREAMING MIND CREATES

THE ANNALS OF JACK KEROUAC—Annals indeed—anal ones—the Mind wished and dream'd itself a spate of San Jose where I'm taken to the parking lot of work at a location I hadnt daydreamed, on that road leading North from Santa Clara towards the yard office and the airport—and because I'm not drinking or smoking tea my mind is very clear and I'm very friendly and direct with everyone and play with the kids with a spirit of serenity etc.—gray but happy scenes, at the lot, where Evelyn drives me, and and I see the cars, the departing park-er, the boss, etc. —but the Mind loses control in a scene in a toilet across the street from Cody's house and Cody and I are taking craps side by side in a double crapper, Cody is talking about an actor as I wipe myself with paper, he says "But you know he's queer, he blows the Kings" and I have my part on my lap while wiping myelf, it's naked, and at the mention of these erotic matters I can feel the swelling so I hurry to wipe up ere it's a pole but get all tangled in the wiping and get some crap in my mouth, a piece, for some reason with paper and reaching in and pieces that get stuck and logics about teeth—here I am surreptitiously trying to remove the hunk of dreamcrap from my mouth which is also full of toilet paper (I'd wiped it instead of below) and Cody's talk about blows is, there's me coming up and I try to hurry, a Comedy—I even dreamed of the taste of the dreamcrap, which is a sensation I can remember only in conjunction with the possibility of a tasteless peanut butter like that 'peach meat' the barrel bug was moulding his way through last week—Meanwhile Cody doesnt notice my dilemna and I'm not working on the railroad so aint worried bout time—

DRIVING INTO THE PICNIC GROUNDS with Mr. Calabrese, little Luke and Ma and others I reach out of the car and grab some brown or yellowish coconut string meat and eat a handful, playfully—it's disagreeable soapy —also the officials of the Park have seen me and are questioning ('reprimanding') me, and Mr. Calabrese who'd already been very sore about 'taking what dont belong to ya' is now redfaced silent about my casually helping myself to the park coconut pile—the first park cop (in civvies) is a middleaged tall sheriff-like Okie in glasses— "Why did you do it?"—I sit in the car alone, parked by the bird house between it and other buildings, the others having gone to enjoy the games, and listen patiently and a little sarcastically to these 'reprimands'—consequently the Sheriff goes off and another Reprimander comes, this a darkhaired man in a blue suit with little mustache—Alternately on his face I see twitching from slick to tough (polite and to outright rough) as he talks to me ("Why?") and tries to figure out whether he should treat me as a member of polite Sunday-driving families (O the time the dog bit me on that Sunday drivegrounds!) (1930)—I watch him warily, consider if he does hit me he will be tough to handle, and dangerously brutal, but I'm ready and wait, feeling only one slight twinge of doubt as to my personal safety & capability—Before, it was the mind wandering its characters around some holiday boulevard like the boulevard of the Garver Farver Hotel of the World and earlier yet, Ma and I are in a plane landing and I'm so afraid it will crash (it _is_ crashing, the Pilot has said for everybody to hang on) and it's that Lilley Lakeview field (Laurier

Field) and also New England Boston Canal Bridge West with Mattapan Charley Rooftops and the Hostess, the lights of streets below, Night—My mother and I are arm in arm on the floor, I'm crying afraid to die, she's blissful and has one leg in pink sexually out between me and I'm thinking "Even on the verge of death women think of love & snaky affection"—Women? who's dreaming this?

SEURAT—the boomcloud pang pock boats

IT SEEMS THE BEAUTIFUL MADE-UP DARK FRESH BEAUTIFUL PEACHES is coming out of the hall room with the high door and transom and with her is a Lesbian, probably Ricki, and so stunning & Maggie-like and darkly beautiful I involuntarily open my arms to embrace her but check myself and Peaches says "Hmf, if you're going to do what you like then why dont you ever?" and haughtily or that is indifferently leaves with the Lesbian—I've been in that room all night, ages, gray anxiety, it's located in the City but what an Aunt Anna dead Gerard lost truck frontporch soft soap gray city, and how lost forever in my recall and forgot even that...as if I'd gone back to Heaven for my old shoes—only final contemplation will upheave the details of that lost life and I write it—

IN SOME LUNCHCART I've just had a big hassel with some people behind the counter—"casting my tears everywhere" I say to myself in trying to recall details and falling asleep on it—anyway I feel sad and broken and suddenly two stools from me sits down a customer, unexpected in the middle of our hateful tragedy, comic in arriving but nevertheless a real flesh customer in our real-life diner—and it's W. C. Fields, !!! I am completely amazed, red nose, strawhat, Fields himself in real life has just happed to wander in—so unexpected and opening such fields of redemptive and cleansing humor I let out a joyful quivering sob involuntarily and W.C., hearing me, only partially glances and politely as if sadly scans the menu in respect for what he supposes is a boy crying next to him about something—and this respect and sorrow so funny, he hasnt said a word yet but you know he will—it was the materialization of Old Bull Baloon, the living Fields, just in time for Sorrow—but had I written this dream in its dawn, I would have brought you a message from heaven about W.C. Fields for in heaven it took place—so funny that he thinks I'm crying from trouble and sorrow, he in fact clears his throat quietly, he sits (just come in) minding his own business, he's all adrift in own his personality adventure and here he is led by the nose by fate to our humble mad lunchcart—the incredible troubles and and jokes that have led him here!

——Just then I was wakened from this dream by the cat giving me two touches with his paw, like wolves do in Indian Tales, and the first time Rondidindu ever did this to me, tho he does it to my mother all the time to be let out—in this case he just wanted to sleep with me (or stop my snoring?)

A GYMNASIUM, A REDHEADED GUY, a murder which I witness and then all night go boasting of it—the scene is Columbia campus presumably and Guy Green's around—Truth is, the white ball basket had not yet been out of the view of the upper dwellers of the Fenway balcony when in a war or some kind I came and ran my rod around and matched mind with mind, finding in it the activity anxiety and also I wanted to be a college graduate and tried to imagine where and what benefits would accrue from a Diploma— skip't the Army, ran out of town, saluted no flags, hid in the basement, made love to dark dolls, practised dhyana in a Burma Cave—"Owk the Kerouac &

here he is, & Told," & I'm going around and make several pointed jokes about the famous war redhead murder which I witnessed in the reeds weeds and knives of a sunny battlefield out by Phillipine Park where the 3 Soldiers saw Snodgrass eating pussy and the Phellipaeen Kings came laying straw mats for the wounded Faustian Heroes of Moody Street and the West End Bar, a big huge grondualted I framshant hassel the size of all the dize wize nizers in the Potterst—cram! crash! crackcizy!—night followed sun,—I saw Guy, maybe Carlo the Porto Rican Hero, maybe Garden of whom ashcans of Henry Afghanistan St. and pink slip front-to-the-West bedroom murders of the sea, and Yucatan Blues (now)—the Vision of the red rust sun park gym all laid out in mem o ry—writ in its proper language—

(Speaking of 'Jeannes' and harking back to the second dream back t'other night is was that incorruptible hot soft and wet gash of Jeanne Desmarais as she after long egrets and egressive forderols finally comes and lays on my Richmond Hill couch (in the livingroom) and I reach down and there it is ready to work, all lubricate—but first I must go to the toilet and leak and it's 6 A M and I wake up anyway—it's the dark and stank grail of the draven, high in the low dreamdark level cot sea or I mean smot flock blanket bot smot rot ran sea, also, can, ran, the Price of the Szelnicks is money changers of the Oogoo Temple—I dont like the hidden sewer dank and holy's saved by scaramooch—as all children ye are—

Revelations of the loose mind in Essence connection—)

WORKING IN THE OUT-OF-TOWN RIVER WATERFRONT as strange longshoreman on the edge of a pier directing the dropdown crane to its vat where protein peanut Oil is churned, and to do so here I am acrobatin on the outside of the rail and over the water and it is the same water of the waters of the 1942 Dream of Brooklyn Liberty Ship Pier which I dream'd because I had thoughts and fears of going back to sea, was being deceived by Iron Irrealities in the Discriminated Lapless Dark of the World and dove, or jumped ship, or suicided, and also as if with Julien on our Last Day...those waters, but in sultry Mississippi South—bunch of stevedores on the opposite slipside are laughing and watching me as I teeter and balance and wave for the dropt down rowboat to guide it—

RETURNED FROM THE HOSPITAL WITH EDDY MAC-ARTHUR (!) (little Irish chum, and from the Gen. MacArthur artilleries) we come to my house on West St and I sneak around the back to see if anybody's home, going thru the motions of darting low in the high dry crackly grass beneath the windows but actually floundering in a semi-effort to bend down head below window levels and not bending nor rushing with any vigor and making a lot of noise—looking into closed windows like the window of the livingroom (dark, like black water) with its linoleum and leather-thickwood furniture and mahogany radio—I blatter down the backyard like this, along the wood fence which is like the yard at Joe Fortier's the day I played the water games around and around his house while he worked at grown-man repairs—I see the little white doghouse—small woodshed in the (now Phebe Ave like) yard and see it's got too many windows, openings, to be secured against winter winds for my inhabitation and it's too small—come around, ring the bell and rattle the screendoor, "front," but on a scaffolding to the left, and high,—I see Eddy Mac waiting out front and Jeanne Desmarais and a girl answering my summons (in shorts is Jeanne)—they say "Your Pa is gone to get his briefcase" but since I've so far only thought of my Ma I assume because they dont mention her she's in the house, maybe sick in her bedroom—I was too lacksaidaisical to be real Indian in my sneak, nothing was real enough—the hospital was a madhouse somewhere

Death the bony owner—

SICK THROAT DREAMS, some virus that makes me swallow and swallow and it gets worse as I feel my throat's not there, as if cut out, so the swallowing swallows void and the more I try to swallow the worse it gets....dreams that accompany this are of the infinite never-ceasing painful karma-activity of the discriminating brain picking up its harsh matter and tormenting out its cold subjects (which we keep calling life)...scenes in a Brooklyn like slum naborhood, everytime I swallow it gets bigger, more complex, more painful...hoodlums, a lot of Sunday dawn action...in front of a poolhall-club at night, the big tree across the street, some of the details I remember (they are of a 'San Luis Obispo dream' nature)...high up on a scaffold with Hal Hayes and little Hal Hayes as we're detected by the cops we start jumping to safety but little Hal jumps right down to the ground a hundred feet below—'No No!' I say as I watch him fall feet first...he seems to land unconcerned and safe in the sand, among a crowd—I keep wanting to be just clear and restful but Karma keeps grinding out these restless images, actions, I swallow in pain and it doubles like a hatching cell, the darkness multiplies, I see now how the mind should be (and is) and how Karma must end—Later Eisenhower or someone is in need of hot water in the upstairs of the Carolina school-Hall so I go down to the cellar where Deni Bleu's been washing and get some water in a bucket—In the sunny green field, beyond the redbrick school I want to buy a lot for my Ma's trailer, ask a farmer in a car, a sheriff—Time's in the redbrick clock—At night in the surprisingly busy backstreets of the little Rocky Mount town I pass the broom wholesaler in his truck, young, and two old broom retailers arguing with him from the street, I see a pack of brooms seven for 29¢—choking on life I see that the stuff of Karma is in Chinese called GHAT—it makes upon itself multiplying, in pain & sorrow—Where's everybody?—After Little Hal jumps, I fall, and as I fall and see the great height I realize this fall will kill me—Previous to going to sleep I'd daydream'd strangely of hitting flat on my face & belly in a fatal fall from high, daydream'd the double flapthwack of brainpan digging brainpan slapping itself to death—the GHAT gets formless but still as yet more torturous—I get embroiled in GHAT entanglements of a hell underworld and wake up suffering, sick, take an anahist because my swallowing is feeding on swallowing and leaving me greater and greater need to swallow—Finally, as the pills work, round 2 P M, I with the window open and fresh air in dream of the 'Gabor Sisters'—one invites the other to join her in Australia while she gets her divorce—I see they'll refuse to recognize decay let alone awful GHAT and be 2 blondes smiling and yakking and being busy and active till they get oldish and fattish and still they'll pretend it's not happening and go smiling and clacking on busy lady heels to stores and finally they will be old and still wont believe that such a thing as sorrow has et them up, living continual self-deceptions with a smile and cosmetics to hide their horror—marrying, divorcing, remarrying—being the famous gay sisters to the world—ZaZa and Eva—never admitting their pain, horror, suffering, despair, evil old age, disease & death ...the fruits of Karma, the rot of GHAT—pretending everything is the same,—being Rumanian Slavic types a la Chekhov, that is, "weeping" instead of understanding.. ...that life is not worth living and they should never have been born will be their final secret thought in the moment of the only deliverance possible to people like that, death —poor fat shams with grown-old gams and gumming yams —blamming around in this World of Clams

I put ashes on the original
And it disappeared.

BRUE MOORE and I are at 59th St Boys Jazz Club and we're going down to the Bowery to light fires in alleys and he'll play his tenor horn—but it's sad October in the night—cold, lost—

LOST BIKES, LOST LOWELL MOONS—Lupine Road nightclubs—girls all night, all kinds—I'm sent to see the girl I'm going to marry' in the little village of Salem witches, she lives across the road near the town square, I knock, a big well built ugly broad answers the door and I think quickly 'O well she's built—really beautifully'—but it's not she, it's 'she's' landlady—my 'she' is in the back, in her own room, humble, is pale, thinner, I cant get a good look at her yet because the landlady is bitching about how far in the room I can stay, how long, though they're both young—My girl has a definite personality, I see the side of her pretty but pale, slightly pimply face and I think 'And she's very sad, and retired, like a schoolteacher, like Bev Watson almost' (lying on afternoon couches in countryhouse rooms)—

It all erupts into a gigantic party at the foot of Lupine Road—I'd been up there, asking questions of Ma about my childhood—now, on Lakeview, the big hotel is having an orgy, you can see couples rushing in and out, they're dancing on the secondfloor marquee, smoking reefers—crowds of toughs hang around the entrance—I'd been away awhile at the Brooklyn pier where Joe and I each had a separate Merchant ship and slept across the slip from each other though at one time during the night in my scary bunk I suspected someone'd come on board maybe Joe—now I've returned to the Lakeview house where the old man had died that Stonewall sunset, events in there—I rush up the stairs of the orgy hotel and knock on a door, inside's a naked colored tall beauty and a man, she rushes out to talk in the hall and instantly I grab her and pull her muff up, holding her pliable fine rump, and she responds and we almost do it right there but it aint time—She too has a definite personality, tall, knows me, calls me a pet name—I run down in the dream and borrow a bicycle and pedal down the Californias to my home—Evelyn's been away, hasnt cooked supper for Cody and the kids—Cody is Joe, I borrowed his friend's bike—At the station I yell at the ticketseller thinking he's short-changed—'O I thought the ticket was 45¢!'—absurd idea, it's $1.65 to the city—I laugh, run out before the change and the ticket are ready, to check on my bike realizing it wont be there, it's stolen—In the gloom I search, search, sometimes finding old bikes without wheels, skeletons of bikes but not mine,—In the weeds...It's the backside of a sad place I've known—I come back to the ticket station, its lights are out, as I come the little street has feet of sleepers sticking out of drapes and I have to be careful—Upstairs in the redbrick apartment I see the lit windows of more girlfriends—What will they say when they've learned I lost the bike! I look for the ticketstation light, fumbling in the dark, there's a light in back where probably the seller's still waiting with ticket and change, on duty, joking with late other men—

By the time I'm in the library and I see the the white ass of the colored girl wiping herself in the shed toilet, and have found my old junks I'd left under the fiction shelf—nameless semi-rubberbands and semi-foods—all the forms the Dharmakaya One-Essence assumes, in these raving human dreams—this raving human Dream this world—While looking for the bike in the weeds a kind of moist bee-like pebble fell into the side of my shoe and I walked on anyway, thinking, "It's wet, I hope it isnt a living bee—it's probably a wet fruit or a wet pebble"—and I left it in—and it warmed up—

IN A DISMAL STUDIO ROOM in New York my whole family Ma Pa & Nin and I have taken up quarters and "all got jobs" and here it's night, one dim light burning, we're conversing but it's a weird conversation, it seems I dont realize what I'm doing and involuntarily or carelessly (because not fearing wrath of women relatives and forgotten the father's because he so long gone in death) I'm rolling a stick of tea and talking right at them some wild excited inanities (born of T) they dont even listen to, rather they're discussing me solemnish and my father gets up and says"He's not worried about marijuana? Eh?" and he comes over to my side—I see him coming and I go blind, darkness takes the place of the entire scene, nevertheless now I feel his touch on my arm, he may have an axe, he may have anything and I cant see—I fall fainting dead in the darkness, with a groan that wakes me up and prevents me from being found dead (if there is such a thing as death) in my bed in the morning—for my blood stop't beating when that Shroudy Traveller finally got his hand on me—He's getting closer & closer—I know how to be beyond him now—by not being concerned not believing in either life or death, if this can be possible in a humble Pratyeka at this time

AFTER READING ABOUT THE TRAGIC REDSUN LOVERS who got lost on an iceberg at Islip Drownpond by floating out to sea later to be saved or discovered when they crash into a lover yacht, and reading about the great Michigan football team which included Keith Jennison, the final paragraph of the football Liberty Magazine article enjoyed only by waiters in dentist's offices dismally with pain to hide, telling of the great defensive backfield play of Jacky McGee, I find myself with the team flying from New York to "Detroit" in a jet plane—Also I'm reading a clear, well illustrated article about jets showing jets shooting off spurts, and spurt-holes—the whole team neatly suited and tied in plush seats, as we come into Chicago and below I see familiar monuments and vast gray avenues of pain and well known dream location I say "Chicago! Hey look we're already in Chicago in one hour!" but everybody is so blasé about airplanes and I'm trying to tell the Aislewashing Attendant Pilot but he's too busy with his pail—We're landing at the airstrip but suddenly it's not an airstrip at all and nobody said we were s'posed to land in Chicago ("Air travel would be much safer if you didnt go landing around everywhere!" I think petulantly)—It's road outside town in a vast park, a straight road but here comes a bus—it moves aside a few feet for us—we make a perfect 3-point landing, no bump, but we're going 200 M.P.H. on that damn road, a straight road though—the bus keeps going its own way casually, it's a kind of brown Macy's delivery bus—Here comes a car—the pilot with his special cynical face as though he was communist deliberately landing us at Chi to create a confusion, swerves aside close to the soft shoulders for the car and I picture us flip flopping over but we dont—My belt is tight on but nobody is concerned, leastwise the aislewasher standing in the aisle smiling—"You'll have to lay over till 3 this afternoon and get a plane via Porto Rico to Detroit" I hear, and it makes me mad to think this is all deliberate airline employee union confusion—We're landed.

LUNCHCART HANGOUT OF FUTURISTIC TEENAGERS somewhere in a room in Lower Centreville Lowell near the confluence of Aiken & Lakeview where lately I've been getting so many dreams of futuristic events and excitements (the Four Brothers, the angered father of Peru), big structures like pyramids in wood out on a sad Surrealist Worlds Fair plain—Deni is showing me a postcard he just received from my mother reprimanding him for his recent attacks on me—It is drawn in pictures, showing vehicular arrangements of people sitting and riding and their positions among the symbols and signs she's drawn—There are 2 other people, a couple—But suddenly I get the tremendous piercingly clear idea: "Deni, always unpredictable in that tremendous gamut he runs, as if innocently between malice and sweetness, is very impressed and looks at me with almost frightened eyes"—"the house you were born in?—you hear that?" he says to the couple—And, because I've just realized I'm back home in hometown Lowell, I get a clear vision of myself going up Lilley and over to the cemetery at Hildreth then down into the Fellaheen Mystery of the wooden tenements down Aiken to Lakeview to the wooded hill of Lupine so bloodsoaked in lore sun in my brain—at the same time I catch suspecting that I'll never really go but hang around gabbing with these people—I live in Pawtucketville across the river and this walk will be on the way home—It's 4 P M sun outside—Suddenly it's night and I aint done it—

TWO BIRDS START FIGHTING AT MY EAR on Bridge Street over the river, they increase their fury and are screaming and biting and scratching with a furious eerie lunacy—they'll end up picking my brains thru my ear

IN THE HALLWAY OVER TEXTILE LUNCH he's come, the Shrouded Traveller who followed me across the desert in 1945—he stands, in an ordinary white shirt, looking at me without expression—it's late at night and the light is on in the wooden tenement hall—He wants to reach out for me—

These 2 dreams are madness & death

HORRIBLE! Aunt Jeanne of Lynn is staying at my house over the Textile Lunch just as I'm coming in and undressing with Maggie Zimmerman for a ball—we're in the kitchen among litters of clothes, boxes—"Why dont you go away!" I yell at the old intruder who is watching us—"I will not!"—I'm undressed right in front of her, lead girl to my bedroom—In there we start—I hear Aunt Jeanne still yakking and threatening in the kitchen—"If she comes in this room we'll go right on paying no attention to her"—But suddenly I feel like insulting Aunt J, and when she addresses another complaint at us (and girl couldnt care less) I say "I'm not Jack—that's not who it is—it's Noël" (her son)—"O Noël, is it" she says ominously "We'll see about that" and she goes to the phone to call my mother at the shoeshop—"Go ahead you old interfering fool!" I yell—When my mother comes home I'll have my bag packed and just take off—after I'm finish't with girl—

WHERE GOETH THE SPIRIT OF THE LIVING? that I should dream I'm going up 2nd Avenue in New York on a cool Summer night among the glittering lights, by bars where crowds of men all look up beer-in-hand at the TV fight, where boys play in the street and bump against me as I walk on hunching my shoulders to show how tuff I am —where to? what final light ahead?

A MAN TIED AT A STAKE to be killed, the executioner sticks two little slivers of steel in his belly which doesnt hurt the man as much as he thought it would so that he waits expectantly, without pain, in curiosity and silence—but the wretched executioner has a thin smile, pulls out a gadget like a vegetable grinder or like a tin toaster that you put on stoves over the heat and lay the toasts on the 4 sides—it is a pre-arranged hooker for the 2 slivers of steel, an ingenious, ghastly, murderous invention of the beast himself—As the victim watches, still with that heartbreaking lamblike expectant curiosity he steps up, hooks the 2 slivers in the inside of the tin gadget, and pulls up—Some action takes place to Hara Kiri the man's entire guts, he lets out a gurg of horrified pain and twists up, tied, and dies—head falling down—

AT A TEENAGE HANGOUT of Village nightclub on 14th St near 5th Avenue in the strange New York night I'm with Ma, who wanted to come along—But it's a dim Apache sinister place and she's out of place but curious—A beautiful redhead is sitting with me in a booth with two other guys, one of them like Tod of Easonburg, big, thick, quiet —The girl throws two quarters on the table saying "Anybody wanta f--k?"—I leap at the chance, but there's some understanding that Tod is supposed to make it also (the 2 quarters) but he doesnt move so without looking at him and without having bought any beer I pick up the nearest beer bottle and up-end it and drain it and slide out of the booth pulling the girl—We are walking down 14th Street at 3 AM towards Deni Bleu's pad, Ma is with us, tired—she wants to sleep—I suddenly realize I have no right to bring people to Deni's in the middle of the night—"Better go home on the subway to Queens" I tell Ma—she's too sleepy, doesnt want to—the redhead is now a nonchalant Maggie Zimmerman walking along quietly with me—Next thing you know I'm all alone on the El in the vast lost Brooklyns, got so many things and junk I'm carrying and some ice-cream-fruit-salad-and-vegetable salad oil slopped together and melting in a carton, but good—I spill some on my shirt and am wiping it when (now a bus) the bus pulls up at Richmond Junction Stop—I wipe while the man next to me struggles out via my knees—Then I gather all my junks, my teamster transfer and rush to the front just as the last little girl is getting out—"Hey,—I'm getting out here!" I yell but the driver wants to screw me up and drives on, fast, flapping the doors shut—I yell and struggle down the aisle —He refuses the transfer on some grounds I cant hear—the passengers seem to be on my side and are yelling me instructions—The busdriver insanely shouts "I heard you say so-and-so, you were trying to bribe me, I'm going to have you hauled in the police court—"

"Stop the goddam bus!" I shout seeing now he's just a nut—He gets red in the face—"I'm gonna have you fined and put away"—He momentarily is frightening me with his imposing legal and busdriver authority threats—But I say "Stop so I can get out here!" and I dont have time to tell him I've got too much stuff to struggle ten blocks back with but he goes even faster—So I up and shove my heel in his face just as everybody's going to scream and the bus is going to careen—and wake up, my heel kicking in the air—of the bed—

FATHER & SON EPIC, finally (me) the father is hopping freights East and meets his 10 year old son doing same thing— "His face so covered with soot the father cant recognize him"—I am the little boy as well as the father—It's a place like Santa Margarita, in the mountains, a grove of woods across the track—A freight train is heading into a siding and I'm (with my pack) trying to decide the best way to get on so it wont be going too fast for the baby

—I'm running at a slow dog trot for his sake, almost a slowmotion dogtrot—I waited too long because the freight headed in gathering momentum after the throwing of the switch by the head man but now it's balling thru quite fast, a long siding, I see that the hotshot passenger is already balling by the upper switch and I get a dream fear the freight will just hiball the gate and go on—everything compressed and speeded up—but lo, even so, another freight is coming down the mainline behind the passenger so we'll have plenty of time to get on and I pick the second to last car which is abreast of us now, doors open—There is no caboose on the rear of this spectral train—At this moment as I'm running slowmotion to the open car with the kid I hear shouts and see two dirty roughlooking bums hightailing it out of the grove of trees with unmistakable intention to beat me for what I got in pocket & pack—I have money folded in my back pocket and stuff of value in the heavy pack along with my lost blue halftoothbrush which proudly I've allocated to my extra pants—"I have no knife!" I think with horror, no defense, no rocks—As if alone, gibbering in haunted world, I start running down a pebbly hillside but stop realizing they'll catch me with my slow pack—I think of throwing rocks but they can throw em back—I think of running for the open car but it's stopping now and all this will happen in the passing roar of the other freight hiballing alongside so nobody in the world can hear murder and I think with horror of the impression this will make on the heart of the little boy—I'm all tangled in the molasses of self dream—wake up wishing I could be Buddha and have no fear of selfhood, of the dissolution of self, of pain and insult and death—

If God were real everything would be honey
And so everything is honey truly

A VICIOUS WAR with all the American infantrymen continually blasting away with their rifles but I'm the Company Joker Imbecile who's always losing his gun and looking for another that works so in the midst of battle (on ramparts, hills, in copses, against enemy soldiers hiding) you hear me yelling "Where's my gun hey?" and everybody too busy to pay attention or even laugh—My sadsack soldier role—But at one point I look up and realize the vast ruin of a European town we're in, the architecture of the town clearly seen in the rubble—I'm lost and cant find my company, no one cares, it's a huge new war—

AIRPLANE DISASTERS (in this same war) have been recorded by a camera device that takes pictures of people while they're crashing you see their agony and even one shot of a man rolling over in smoke—(at the crash)—the device never breaks—We're watching a series of pictures—I am completely horrified because I identify myself and forget it's a (dream) device taking the pictures—Civilian passengers are shown in a writhing tormented assembly in the brave brown plane as it's hurling downward in the night to crash and kill them all—You see men looking at one another with expressions of intolerable regret—I watch one man looking down at the floor quietly—as the others moan and pray and writhe—He is going to allow the crash to take him quietly—But as the picture goes on, closer and closer to the actual contact moment of death as the plane nears the ground, our hero has jumped up and is shouting—No matter who you look at, the face (women, children, men) shows something never seen before on that face and never to be seen again—Intolerable regret and great bemused understanding streaked with pale sashes of fear so great I myself tormented to see it—You see shots of the dying in the smoke and flames, famous heroes in throes of agony alone not knowing their pictures are being taken or that anyone will ever see this or that anything will ever happen again—It's the Loneliness of Death, the selfhood of death—the fruits of self at last and the pain and terror of it—Its hold was so great, the letting go of it is a great terrified wrenching—O if I could only describe those faces, the eyes at last looking with a new, a final realization of something—Their throats gulping when they try to take it quietly, some sobbing in hands as the poor world falls screaming to destruction—Og—OM! Deliver all sentient beings with thy diamond mace!

IN A YARD SO VAST are Joe and I when I'm to go get something at the house it's a long trek across the lawn on which scattered gangs of boys are playing long fungo—shouting remotely—Joe and I were sitting against the wire-fence when a stranger in a suit showed up and we both said 'Isnt that Dicky Hampshire'? tho because he was lost at Bataan we dont take our supposition seriously—Darker and bigger it is Dicky—"I knew it was you by the back of your head"—There is no elation of reunion or rediscovery just serious handshaking and calm Bhikku gravity and aloofness—Joe is "grown up" and well combed and big—Later we're in my Sarah Yard and then something happens to the dream whereby I take and remove a wall of my mother's house to the other side of the street to "make more room" but now traffic interrupts the house and you never wanta go for water (to the kitchen) across all that traffic—There are 4 little Pinky kitties in the grocery store, I gather them cursing—I want to rearrange the wall and the furniture and the house together again before Ma gets home from work—that long dry tired lawn—

A DOUBLESIZE TRAILER some people had (packwagon) which is really a big useless Trailer with wood rails and no top, wanted to sell it to Ma and me—They stopped at our roadside house on the sunny dirtroad of the Old Shrouded Arab Dream—I advised Ma not to buy it—But these people were Okies Old and had an old man with em on whom I felt it incumbent on me to take pity so I mixed him a ice n water jug in the kitchen but it seems the ice is wine-encrusted or soaked and the glass jug is full of red portwine, so I plan on telling the travelers that I've made them a pot of Wine Water with Ice, a big glass at that and their dusty road travails'll be nil—The old man with white hair, I worry about him, I struggle to get the wine outa the ice cause I really want to help, refresh and please him—the hot sun is shining, it's summer in the Dream

I'M LOOKING IN THE MIRROR at my back molars and I can yak out my whole toothiness jaw so's ya can see like the skeletal hint of what's to be, the leer of bone teeth—the Molars are huge and have a single verticle dirty line running down em that makes me sick shudder to think Ive grown so old-&-decayed & am such a skeleton—I snap my jaw back in

EVERYBODY MOVES WITH A STAMPEDING ROAR when the time comes for all to go en masse to the great World Premiere in the rain but there's only one car, one coach train car, at the door, admitting just so many, & the car is soon full, fact I dont even see it fill or anyone get in, & the Public Address shouts "That's enough, that's the first load" and he's been working everyone up to a frenzy of excitement to get to the Premiere and now it'll take all night to even get the people there let alone raise the curtain on the first rainblear brownmoth mask—I see the theater, the night, the marquee, the empty street, the one vehicle coming like a worm in the Science Fiction or Crazy Mad Comic Night to discharge Martian Lilliputian passengers, First Nighters yet—"We'll all go!" is the shout in the Tortured Hall—I've been wreagling all night to wrongle myself a wrass to get in—Write!

I'M AT MY RAINY MORNING WORKDESK in shroudy Manhattan and I look down by the dock and see the Navy vessels anchored in the bay and the crowds of sailors walking on the water towards the land—I say "Everybody's learnt that trick now—it seems to be easy—too easy—it must be some simple gimmick"—

MICKEY MANTLE, he's on TV, at bat, the bat's in his hand when the fight starts and you see the cleancut young America Hero swinging the bat right at the guy's legs, cutting him down, you see flailing white uniformed ballplayers, explosions of violence on the screen

VERY AFFECTIONATE OLD DREAM OF HAL HAYES, Kafka novels, Raphael Urso studying, in the library, rows of books—Hal has a vast shelffull of books of all kinds, plus voluminous huge personal notes on music handprinted by him painstakingly in ink in vast ledgers that some hoodlum-type or boss or ambiguous intruder is leafing thru and wondering out loud, as Hal & his girl humbly watch—"Wow, is that poor Hal studying!" I think. "He knows as much about music as Nietzsche"—Meanwhile Raphael is reading by another shelf, head bent—I see the exciting bright covers of The Trial and The Castle by Kafka, I want to take The Trial home and start an interesting new year of reading & study—I feel very happy—the air is cool, Autumnal when I wake up—

GIANT ROCK SUPPORTING THE ENORMOUS BEAUTIFUL CATHEDRAL of the World of Notre Dame in Montreal-Lowell near the South Common and Ma and I and someone else (Hal Hayes?) are looking for a Chinese

Street Ste. Catherine Restaurant to eat our big gay shopping dinner, it's around Xmas and the scenes in the dusk are glittrous, the mountainous rock, the steep cliff where I'd been in a long ago dream and feared of falling to the flats below (the dream of workin railroad on cliff above red-brick town, Montreal yet also leading off to dusty roads to Mexico—& also I'd walked up there along a rickety broken fence, right on the edge, the buildings in the moon-light like Joe McCarthy's buildings in the training grounds and General MacArthur's Hospital Buildings, all these scenes in a Complete World to which I try to give a mortal sense of name)—Very happy when I wake up, to put my day-shoes on—and read Chuangtse

GOING THROUGH AN ABANDONED HOUSEBOAT or muddy apartment on the side of the river with Danny Richman I steal an old victrola top and take it with me to town, where it's played but doesnt work too good and has to be wound—goes unnoticed in the general rack and ray of city excite-ment—There are movies, Ma and I get in—I'm sitting on the ground, a guy goes by staring at me curiously then sees my mother and they fly into greetings—he wears glasses—Going back up the river with Danny along the bank I'm mindful of how when the Yangtse floods you cant tell a horse from a cow on an islet and I look out to the Mississippi islets—dots—it's warm, the grass and bank-side is warm, bugs, I worry about ticks, we cut along the levee grass, walking back America—we go through that houseboat again and I think of stealing the victrola but I've already done that—Afternoon sun rays in goldenly through the ruined windows—

MONTREAL, RUSSIA. Big scenes with parents in a build-ing, involving the shiftless brother-in-law Eddy Jones, who is a taxidriver lush in this strange dark Northern

Gloomtown—All drizzly and gray it is, as Eddy and I who am 18 years old and still kid-like, start out in his cab to get something—Eddy's like a thin W.C. Fields—"Boy" he says "wait here till I get me a shot of whiskey—Now the trouble with your folks is, they're always pesterin somebody to do dis and do dat—What I like is my freedom, see?—" He goes driving all over town and finally at drizzly dawn on some street in the Russian Flats and whorehouse district outside town he comes up to a gigantic Street Paver Machine that takes up the whole road and is four foot high with racks for tar, run by an old workman—Eddy rams his cab right into it, brang, and the whole thing shakes and quivers and moves forward, not heavy—Eddy's having a big time and laughing and is drunk & crazy—Next he rams up against a panel truck and keeps pushing it back (it's empty) towards a pedestrian who's trying to walk in the street—and because the wheel is turned the truck follows the man in an arc—a panel truck or cab earlier also pushed, out of which leaps now a visored driver drawing out an evil looking revolver with a wood handle—"Hey" I say from the back of the cab "I'm only a passenger, take it easy"—he holds it by the barrel to use it as a slugger while the pedestrian has already rushed up and hauled Eddy out of the cab and is bopping him hard and professionally on the chin with his fists so I rush up to stop it and do so by yanking Eddy from the punches and holding him at my side—Just as the taxidriver's about to lodge <u>his</u> complaint the pedestrian to my surprise removes a gun from his pocket and calmly shoots Eddy one shot in the chest—Eddy is surprised and feels the pain only afterwards, and falls—I'm suddenly alone with him on the dismal windswept drizzly street of dawn, not a working street and so not a person in sight up and down the gray reaches of its dimness—Eddy is writhing and crying "Get me a shot of whiskey"—"But where? how?"—I find myself all alone with a man whose injury may be serious but I cant tell and he wants whiskey and lies in the road in pain, sentimental, my crazy drunken uncle-in-law—I'm so embarrassed I wish I could go away—(But on the corner there's an allnight whore and gambling cocktail lounge, with blue curtains in the plush door)—"I'll go there and get a shot of whiskey Eddy?"—"Yea, yea, but get a whole bottle, you'll spill the shotglass bringin it back—"—I feel in my pocket, I have just a $5 bill and I think "For poor wounded Eddy I can spend that final fin" but I get twinges of guilt and remorseful fear and greed-anxiety and hear myself saying "Have you got $5"—"Yea, yea, in my pocket, get it there" and he can, I have to feel in his pockets because he cant turn over and I look up to see if anybody sees me, thinking "They'll think I'm a mugger rolling a guy"—bills fall out, I take a 5 and rush to the corner in the gray mist, go in the bar—They wont sell me a bottle—"Its too late, what the hell's the matter with you, dont you know that?"—It's dark in there, plush, blue, gold bar bottle lights and a dim piano in back and a few voices of people who've been drinking all night till dawn—I want to tell them why I need the bottle—They're talkin among themselves—"Gotta wait till 8, city ordinance"—I get furious at the world with its goddam rules and comment about rules and there's my uncle dying for a drink in the rain with a bullet wound in his chest, I grab a bottle off the shelf at the end of the bar and run out fast —"Let em chase me! Eddy'll get his drink!" but as I reach the partitioning curtains I dont hear a commotion on the other side, they're still commenting about the city ordinance and there's even someone chuckling so that instead of being chased and shouted and shot at, I'm completely in the clear with the quart of whiskey and Eddy's $5 bill!—I run out silently and up the street to Eddy—But he's dead—Standing there with the bottle and his five dollar bill in my hands, over Eddy who's just become forever pure, I cry in shame and bitterness

THERE'S BEEN A TOWER SET UP in the city to show where the atom bomb is going to be laid when time comes to blast the city—announcement has been made for next month, and evacuation begun—You see the city at night now, dark, under a dim moon, low lights everywhere from the diminishing and dimming population—I'm there on a sad tenement balcony planning my departure up the northern river to the right—All the Porto Ricans linger yet in doom'd New York trying to salvage one last month of tasting the rich leftovers of a once-rich city—trying to eat up all their Manhattan Love, their Manhattanana, before they have to leave forever—I look at the tower in the moonlight, it looks so sinister, guarded, shrouded, to die—

"RIDING TO PRECISELY THE SAME MUSIC as at the beginning of the picture," the movie ad says, "Turhan Bey is seen entering the crowded city of Havalah—" you see pictures of a tremendous phalanx of easy riders invading an easy city, with turbans on, the plain thereof—then, the "end of the picture" they're fighting sword, tooth, nail and horses' sthump through the narrow alleys of Halavah—"the battles are Narrated by Jewish Commentators" says the announcer—An after battle scene is shown of war prisoners hanging by their hands from public porches and you hear a loud THUMP as in the dimness and streetmoil below the announcer advises you that "a party of executioners became impatient because behind in schedule and cut off the head right on the sidewalk" but I missed seeing that, just heard it—a moily vitriolic city Turban Bey did emancipate—

TRYING TO WRITE ALL NIGHT at the cafeteria booth but wearing big thick Lowell Highschool Track red sweater and also shoulderpads of football, finally I take it all off and Ma who's talking with women friends nearby wants to know if I feel aright—"J ava sho" (I was hot)—Earlier Joe was in that Sunday House in Salem Street standing around longlegged, archaic, like a watcher in old rainy photographs—

"ONE OF THE NICE GUYS OF LOVE, MUSELLE" is a a song someone's singing in a deep dream—

THICK SMOKE IS RISING from the dust heap over across the highway where weeks before we'd laid out some of our rubbish to burn and far from not being burned out it's gotten worse, a dog is barking next to it—Ma, Nin, Pa & Me go across the highway to see, from our big gray screenporch house—it's somewhere in the South—I'm annoyed by the traffic and try to sneak between cars to cross but they keep streaming mindlessly—

Cabooses on a winter morning spurt sweet comfort smoke—

You see the President of the Lions Club sitting among the boys on the balcony as the organ plays "Hold That Lion" and he's got a crewcut now, his split teeth show even more, he's Bill the popular Prez and you see he's conscious of his new haircut and wonders what the people of America'll think of it—The camera swings up to the great ceiling and up to the prison above where prisoners can hear the music and the rally, you see wire caging and gray light—

BACKWARDS FALLING STAIRS and the steps only 3 inches wide—so painfully I'm coming down those, holding to the rail, slow, returning from the auditorium of the Negroes

—It's a moonlit night, it's somewhere, I'm a seaman—A colored acquaintance of mine is walking with a colored girl, they see me—I tell them "Their stairs kill me"—We walk along towards the great Auditorium where I live, where I'd been entrap't earlier for stealing jewelry and the guy wants to make the girl but she's going to a party so he cuts off at a little sidestreet with ruts in the dust and sleeping cottages and I go on with her—Soon I've got her hand in mine and teasing my finger along—She says she's going to a party of six people, at a cop's house—"Are you the seventh?" I say—"I like to feel hands," she says—aint pretty, sorta fat, ugly, but sexy—It's New Britain—When they'd caught me earlier I was way up the giant steps hiding where the blond guy identified me to a plainclothesman, I darted through the embrous awe hall rungladders among echoes of the show, guilt, it wasnt me but my friend started it—gelatinous thefts—Now, walking in the moonlight, the auditorium has become my room and I want to take her up there but she's going to her party

IN SOME APARTMENT IN NEW SHMICAGO I take a desperate leak into an empty pint bottle of Wine because other empty quart bottles have already been pissed full by Hubbard earlier—I realize half with horror in the dream gray humorlessness that it's my own old pint I'm using—I dont want to piss on the floor and create a great noticeable puddle in the girl's pad but so, my piss wells up quick to the neck and overflows welling abundantly and richly and too much all over my hands and down the sides of the bottle and on the hardwood uncarpeted floor—

UNPEARLIED OLD UGLY GRAYDUST TRAIN, the Zipper, ready to go to Watsonville Junction so I get on and roam inside the passenger coaches (!) and then it gets underway but the wrong way, towards the city, so in trying to get off I clamber down the rungs, but my large buncha keys' in my way, keep dangling from my hand and when I try to put em in pocket (while on rungs) they wont go in but dangle half in half out and of course I cant lose em so I hold on precariously with three fingers grabbing the grab-irons and train speeds up tremendously—I get to the point of the Gray Locomotive and come down, turning the ground and the train away from me as I quietly relax off, arm out kissing the rungs goodbye, foot out in heel-up railroader's balance, like a stylized dance it is—off & safe.

IN STRANGE SNOWY FRISCO I got down shortcutting behind Market but end up in the countryside among snow covered farms though they're still 'parallel to Market' but now a closed tunnel seals off my return so me and other guy go through the wood barrier door and come into vast underground caves full of escaped Oriental War Prisoners hiding out—we go on various levels, deeper & deeper more lost, among scrabbles of rock, dust, refuse, papers, crap, dank, drips, leaks, from overhead city—finally I find my two searched-for Orientals over a fire in the corner of the Vast Ah Cave Eternity and if I dont watch out they'll roast me for supper because there's no food down here—O what happened to the snowy farmhouses?

ALLEN EAGER recordplaying in the closed livingroom in Textile Lunch Tenement and I call it to Danny Richman's attention but he not interested—I go in the door and listen, I wish Allen would play louder and more distinct but I recognize his greatness and his prophetic humility of volume, his 'quietness'—I got to go down the gray dank stairs where the Shrouded Traveler had been in white shirtsleeves,—down on the street level I stop and there all my dream life comes back to me in a solid wave, sad, gray, huge,—everywhere unending gray scenes and dismal —this is the price of sentience, the current of deaths and rebirths—O path of sweet Permanency, through what wood, what raindrop?

IN LOWELL I'VE APPLIED TO THE SUN, with Jimmy Santos presumably, for a job on Commentary Magazine and he's written back a big glowing welcoming letter and offering me the job but Ma is leery and says I shoulda stayed low because now that I'll be makin money and makin myself known others'll be wantin it—so I ponder not doing anything at all, svaha!—Meanwhile there's been a play or I wrote or acted a play and the final scene is on with the hero father at the picnic grounds holding a big waterglass full of red wine, well dressed, with wife who says "You drink too much" and I look at Nin and she says "Of course he does—" This man has a son who is arguing with him about big philosophical issues all the time—the man is in a tweed coat—Now I'm with Joanna going up to her room, new room, in a little narrow hall, I go in with her, as she bends to get something I'm pinned by her behind and we push together a little but wanting her to think that I'm not vulgar but appreciative of her sweetness I quickly throw a little kiss on her dress, bending inward down—We then neck sloosily, dreamily—She's very beautiful and I love her—

The lifespan of an ant is very short, and it only learns that learning is ignorance—

Walking into Lowell from the long alienated "north side" not far from that circus cliff of recent I suddenly pass a square which is familiar suddenly as being some old forgotten Lowell place I'd felt alien and never sought to rediscover in my thoughts—somewhere in the mixups of cathedrals, wooden tenements, railroad tracks and heavy traffics back of North Woburn Street and back of

South Common, up towards South Lowell, around to the east, strange—my flash of remembrance is in the dream and _for_ the dream, for now I see there is no such spot in Lowell or in mind but I made it up to fit the dream, showing how the dreamer Mind is not concerned with such arbitrary Conceptions as fantastic or non-fantastic—whether it took place or not, all its thought memories are active, pulling out of absent blue air the empty images of a dreamer world

I'M LOOKING FOR A PLACE to sit and write quietly at the baseball park and go around a fountain and batting cage wire to a bench on the side where there's an old typewriter & desks under a tree and here I turn into "Malcolm Cowley" and start typing—but so old the Machine, to register letters ya gotta hit it one finger at a time _hard_, which I do,—& there's a sad young kid there, of 18, definite personality, curly brown hair, thoughtful, as an interested old Man of Letters I begin to interview him sympathetically and find he's a young tender poet so saddened he doesnt write much, or some such,—walked 2 1/2 miles before I wrote this, so part forgot—So he stares into space in my dream and I worry about him—Who's subjective? Who's objective?

A WILD DREAR EPIC OF A FAMILY living in the far North on a strange high seacoast whose waters come up and lap the doorsill at high tide and in storms lashes the whole house trembling—it's like Alaska, the days are short, darkness predominates—I'm there with Ma & Nin and there's a short sunny summer when we arrive, warm enough and pleasant—"I loved it so much when it came, suddenly one afternoon, six weeks, ago," is saying the old grandmother of the house on a cold sudden dusk, "but now it's winter again"—For awhile too there'd been playing around in the lawn across the road from which begins the whole Ars Scotia Wilderness that goes & goes, solid, all over the Far & Hopeless North—the games in the yard were wild, with white horses and roughplay, I get on mine and chase the boys who've thrown bats at me and tackle them from bareback—it's all in play but wild—Now winter's come back, the house shakes from the blast and roar of the terrifying sea, the seas saw terribly, you see it hungrily licking the kitchen door from gray infinity like Greenland seas north of Cape Farewell—the father of the house is a mad old miser with a servant who hates him, you see them eating together a miserable meal in a barn, by crazy candlelight, in the Alaskan Town—the servant saying "You miserable (fool) all your life has been wasted in this Northern Waste with your silly outcries about the Days of Armageddon and your Bible, making everyone quake because you're crazy"————Suddenly the servant is no longer sitting in his chair next to the Mad Master who is glouring, but in mine, and I am become the servant. Meanwhile I'd been to the Alaskan town, with my girl, the only girl in the country for me—Looking for candy stores to make sure I can get enough gum—gay restaurants with beer and whole families and booths and Community boots and mackinaws, a man sitting on the bar stool with a celery stuck in it by a child—My girl (Maggie Zimmerman) and I wander among the barns of Main Street, the skies are gray iron—Now the master is being excoriated by the servant in the Town barn Last Supper and then the big storm comes and lashes the whole little house and shakes it in night and you know the house is going to be destroyed now and the Master jump up on a high wagon and scream in the gloom about his Prophecy "In the days when the windows be darkened and the daughters of music are brought low—" and he's going to drown in the tide with his slave and you'll hear a Spokesman of the Epic say "Thus they drown'd together, he who lived in, and he who sought to live from, the waters of death" (the second the master, and you see a scene of the wreckage littered Sea) but I'm going to rise up and make a huge speech of my own for the benefit of the hearts of everyone and all the kind grandmothers, girlfriends, aunts I've known in this dear lil house is this drear North, I'll say "Windows-be-darkened-be damned, all he had to do was build his house on higher ground!"—anybody can see

Earlier, or later, I was trying to steal some yellow paper pads from the Western Union desk in the Marble Subway corridor but kept hesitating over how many till finally I decided to steal them all but by then the pretty secretaries began going from room to room though they paid really no attention to me and dug me

IN THAT FATED cold northern town I go from the marble station of events as murky as spiderwebs, to Pat Fitzpatrick's house, day time, to see his wife Marie, for a f., I hope—no one in, I go in, eat a new slab of American cheese off a bedroom sideboard then think to call out "Marie?" and by God she replies from deep in a bedroom and no longer innerested in me as I tell her who I am—So out on the railroad track we're trying to make a joint that'll crack the wood gimmick that's holding us up and my cat Pinky's lying on the railbed watching and as we make a try he comes up and smells the thing we put on—"He'll get run over!"—but the move starts again, and Pinky lays down safe between the tracks, watching, the coolest cat that ever lived—We make the slamming SPROWM joint and Pinky blinks to hear it in his drowse—we make our objective, dust, I pass the sign, wild autumnal clearday winds blow, Marie F. may no longer love me but I got my cat and tag team and works of the Mind—

Later on the passenger train I yell with

glee and amazement when I see the railroad men of a strange local kicking a gon down a dead lead into a derail and over to tumble tragically in a sand hollow, because useless—"They kicked that gon over!"—The brakeman laffs and says "It's because the sides are wore out"—"The slats are run thru"—it's 'Woburn'—'near Lowell'—lots of sand and new construction and wild excitement in the wind whipped day with puffclouds racing in the glitter blue—I think of the randy dark body of Marie in the bedroom and her sultry careless voice—soon we'll be in Lowell and I'll see the heart's desire scenes—a whole book in itself, God—When Autumn wins my heart again and makes me lose my love the trees will take the Dreams, Roads, Dharma Railroads and Bubbles of the Mind Sea and crash them back to Eternity

FRANKLIN ROOSEVELT JR ON TV handing out eggs—and the drug that is sprayed from a strange syringe—Roosevelt sticking his hand out of the TV tube in my house and I reach out and take what he offers, cracked eggs, a big bottle of Accent, garlic salt, Ma and I are talking excitedly as I take and so miss a few times when FDR reaches out a thing and because not taken vanishes into space—I rue the things I missed, gloat to see the ones I got—

————The kid wanted to be friends, we went to the hospital, got shot spray dope from the nurse's syringe, I'm standing there becoming completely drowsy and crazy in front of other patients watching as the nurse administers—It's only later the sailor turns sinister (after our stay in the Sarah Avenue Hospital) and with his friends under the Jamaica El (where the timber fire was in the El) makes suggestive gestures of a fight, how they'll all beat me up, he in the lead and already I got my escape planned

THE UP & DOWN WILDRAMPS of an unbelievable Brooklyn waterfront, with parts rising up like drawbridges and girders among and workers (I have a job, like railroad switching off the floats New York Dock Rwy. but it's a weird darkwork where we communicate across big holes in our upramps and sometimes it's hard to climb they're so steep, you get some kind of pay and overtime according to their steepness)—in night I am wandering, in white t-shirt, looking for my work team, finding spectral buildings like Squibb's or the St George Hotel but just wood mansions full of sleepers, closets, sexes, sheets, dank abandoned rooms—the foreman cant find me—Finally I find June Evans and she immediately wants to blow, on the bottom step of the big Rank Roadramp Tower of Babel—we, she starts—we smile, hurry off—I lose her in the big house though she told me what room she'd be in—I go a floor below, miss her, find her finally much later after ship-like events and loneliness in a maze of lost corridors of the dark mind's house—She's in the sack but a kid is playing in the room and we gotta get him out—She smiles like an angel with radiance from her dark heaven—I wake up realizing all is a dream, especially the Morning Waking—

DREAM OF THE GROWNUP MAN CHASING ME, I'm a little boy in some town somewhere, homeless, I've done some prank or vandalism and he's mad and wants to catch me, wears white shirt like the Shrouded Traveler in the Hall—upon Main Street near the High School he starts chasin me, I run down thru the lawns of the school and over the iron picket fence and down a side street to houses like the houses of Gershom with leafy mysterious yards—There's a sandbank beyond (primal, scene of world red-sun birth) I got my eye on—He keeps coming behind me always about 2 blocks away but persistent and shakeless—

I've really become terrified and have to use every craft of child sneakability to completely escape him or else—he's insane—I go into a house hall, hide, as in old dreams, people inside dont hear me, I sneak around, under porches, in rooms of perfect strangers—the angry grownup is outside looking, looking, he knows I'm near—I sneak out thru bushes to other yards of the dank houses of death, and come to the open spaces of the sand shrub hills there and I take off across a long hollow for the other end—clearly defined country, with water beyond I'm sure, and "seen before"—in a gray north land—he's right behind, has seen me and hurries nearer, knows I would take to the open from fear of houses and yards—What did I do?*****I hide carefully on the far end of the hollow but as he approaches (himself hiding) I know he'll just simply see me—backtrack may lead to ridiculous, going-further may be hopeless, I ponder and breathe hard—There's a lil old house at the hillslope, I invade it and hide among woodslats and wet sound—My Shroud approaches—I know he'll get me (woodslats and wet sound, that's masturbating with the twins at five), he knows too the bastard sooner or later he'll get me but being a kid I have great potentiality and all the world yet and left to hide in and cover with tracks—Shall I go towards the mysterious old Chalifoux woods beyond where woodstumps I was born in redmorning valleys of life hope?—or sneak back snaky into town? (Who the boy? Who chaser?) Who objective? Who subjective? Who real? What real? All liquid phantomry in my mind essence dreaming, like life—Ha!
(Close your eyes to all danger & dont be afraid to die.... it's all imaginary & empty & great)

WITH MY CRAYONS I drew a marvelously beautiful scene of some buildings in late afternoon, maybe churches or stores but using pink and deep inkblue lavishly and very

heavy with the hand I have put up a color of awe and mystery of the late sun on old stone that is so beautiful, something never before seen by human eyes, a work of art worthy of a DaVinci, a Rembrandt even—
—I'm amazed just a little to see I'm a great artist—Unfortunately I drew the picture on the TV screen "during a color broadcast" and now as I'm just about to show it to my mother the colorcast ends and ordinary pale luminous gray faces show and my whole masterpiece is completely wiped away—"Damn bastards changed!" I yell —It was a scene like Venice in the late Fall afternoon, blues & pink & stone salmon & awe gulp dark sorrow that made you think of Jesus & Magdalene

"WHEN YOU CLIMB POLES..." It was a seashore town epic with families, I'm up in a tree or a pole for my own amusement but the father (Mannerly-like whom I just insulted in his attic classroom) cries "Fire! dont you see the fire from up there? When you climb poles—when any of _my_ gang climb poles it's to spot fires and hurricanes" but suddenly he and his brood of brats realize the fire is close to their own house and they start running there and where I am I can see it's their house indeed at that—Finally when the hurricane is coming they send a silent dead boxcar down the long peninsula rail, to block something—my whole life's imaginary worries had all swum by on the gray peninsula—

AT DAWN (after yesterday's initiation of One Meal A day-No Drink-No Friends "Western" device for Buddhism) a namelessly beautiful joy in my dreambrain concerning the Single Taste of all things, a transcendental sensation of Singleness in the Universe, a Solitary Ecstasy—Interrupted by the daily morning vulgar throat-clearing of the Fat Pole next door and yet I blessed him in my happiness and all anger had disappeared——Later my mind went ignorantly deeply asleep & consumed itself with visions of rough seas, seamen struggling with a lifeboat over the side of a freighter & suddenly all disappearing to drown and you dont see anything on the sea till a minute after the floating rowboat hulk 300 yards down the starboard stern, the men gone except for inky seablobs—Earlier I'd been in the old Sun Building in Lowell and asleep upstairs & some man, thinking me drunk, carries me downstairs to Kearney Square & I fake outness, a tender scene, he's got me like a baby—then I walk on up to a lunch cart near the Y and up Merrimac Street and report my story to someone in the dark rainy day—evil weirdness of Kearney Square, the whole thing is nothing but a discriminated cerebral hassel and this I may say for the entire book of dreams of images to disturb its unbroken serenity & preoccupations with imagelessness though <u>how</u> this is so I cant tell yet in words that are in themselves discriminative hassels of arbitrary conception——As I say, words, images & dreams are fingers of false imagination pointing at the reality of Holy Emptiness—but my words are still many & my images stretch to the holy void like a road that has an end—It's the ROAD OF THE HOLY VOID this writing, this life, this image of regrets——————

FOR THE FIRST TIME—dreamed I climbed a gradual cliff from slope to slope and got up on top and sat down but suddenly in looking down I saw it was not a gradual cliff at all but sheer—in the dream no thought of getting down on other side—in the dream as always in Highplaces Dreams I'm concerned with <u>getting down the way I came,</u> or rectifying my own mistakes—and even though I know it's a dream, within the dream I insist I must get down off the high cliff I climbed—the same old fear grips me in mortal throes—"But if it's a dream then the cliff is not real," I tell myself "so just wake up & the cliff will vanish"—I hardly hardly believe it's possible, and trembling, open my eyes & the dream is gone, the cliff is gone, the terror is gone—This is the Sign from Buddha's Compassion at last —In other words, for the first time I dreamed that I was on a high place & was afraid to get down but I knew it was a dream & something told me to wake up & the high place would disappear, & I opened my eyes & it was all gone

SAVED!

Buddha rectified by mistake for me——
AWAKEN FROM THE DREAM

For a moment too I thought of jumping down to get down——O pitiful reality! (but that would mean mortal pain, the falling, mortal horror, or, death)—

Also, in many other Highplace Dreams I knew it was a dream too, but insisted within the dream <u>on getting down</u>—dream-activity in the dreamworld—dream-activity in the dreamworld—dream-action down the dream-cliff—

The cliff seemed to be, and now the cliff doesnt seem to be—

Dream-analysis in only cause-and-condition explanation (such, as, cliff from symbol during waking day, like, murderer with knife because window left unlocked)—dream-analysis is only a measurement of the maya-like and has no value—dream-dispersion has the only value—Freudianism is a big stupid mistaken dealing with causes & conditions instead of the mysterious, essential, permanent reality of Mind Essence—(My only problem is how to practice the Eightfold Path day in, day out, as long as I don't live in solitude—) It's more than just the high cliff of the other-night's-reading-Dante,—it's the high cliff of mortal anxiety—

I'M AT THOREAU'S WALDEN POND HUT in Concord, it's evening and I can barely see as I try to examine some of his mementoe'd remaining personals including a little box of his old smokes, the box made of tearable soft cardboard like that of egg crate layers—a hip chick in a new convertible pulls up and is yanking her emergency brake with headlamps illuminating Thoreau's wall as I yell "Keep your lights on, I gotta see this" because I dig her right away as receptive and cool and I cant see—As she watches over my shoulder I open the box and it's a little thimbleful of marijuana seeds—a little powdered marijuana tobacco, at least seems so and I think "Thoreau was High"—(which is certainly TRUE)—and I tell the girl what it is—She says "That stuff is hard to get"—"Now no it isnt" I say with the authority of a great hipster "you can get it anywhere on the street (from any hustling girl)" I think to add, and in my mind the street is a great Chicago Drag glittering outside Concord & Lowell—Pretty Chick is awed by me—she tears the lil box softly apart for a souvenir, rolling it up into little ball—

(Dream'd in Lowell Skidrow Hotel, the "Depot Chambers")

"COOL IT" I say to a gang of crazy boys I been playin on the rollercoasters with, as one starts shouting loudly about the marijuana exploits I taught them-"Ah hell, cool it yaself" is the answer from my disciples—We're in our shorts and T-shirts, I feel tired of trying to keep up with the consequences of the Beat Generation and all lugubrious in the dream—Wake up in Lowell Skidrow—

'T'is only in the quiet of the Sainte Jeanne d'Arc church on the great gray day of Nov. 21 1954 that I saw: "The Beatific Generation"

AT THE LONG ISLAND GRAYBEACH a big family reunion and event but instead of starting off on time I goof at basketball in the empty Y court, removing coat but not shirt and tie and I'll get all sweaty—I start playing my Self Game, the Kerouacs against the Kraps, the heroes of both sides—I hear juveniles screaming in another court—Then I hurry to the big Confused Event, riding the top of an outdoor subway or freight train right down the Queens Boulevard Mainline and hundreds of other kids are riding with me and it's started to drizzle, the outdoor fireworks at the beach will be a fizzle—The Coach of the Children, Russ Hodges Serious, sees me and calls to me over the boxcars to help a little lost kid by taking him with me—I plan to agree——

THE GREAT ORIENTAL KALIFA is castrating the priests with an expression of tender sorrowful concern, he has a little clasp of silver that he applies to their parts as they go to him opening their flies (but away from the audience so you dont see the actual penises and how it works) but you do see the expressions of disappointed pain on the faces of the faithful who you might expect had thought the Kalifa would rid them of pernicious balls of eros without searing and wounding their conditional bodies so to the quick—I'm next in line, just as reluctant as a dozen others as it dawns on me what castration means—I refuse when glanced at compassionately—It comes at a time when I am about to stop renunciation and begin expecting and accepting everything again—I get up and say "No"—In the next room are the Soldiers of the Brown East, marshalled to overseer the quiet castration of disciples—Two special young brown-skinned guards (not in uniform but like passengers in a Mexico City bus) start whipping themselves up to a frenzy with speeches to each other and then come for me to handle me—But they're ineffectual, I fight them off with that, without even trying and I go to the window and swing out to my escape—One of my old hero buddies who'd been a Monk with me but previous to that a car fixer at the Lowell Depot Garage now makes a speech to the monks and guards of the Kalifa in the tenement funny drowse and rope lines of the court as I drop down on silken cords to the Fellaheen Mystery of Escape "He's such a great escaper, you will note this champion of the world can go down a wall without touching a wall" which indeed I'm doing but without half trying—My escape is clear as air—My enemies have no hold,—My personality is so deficient of self-nature I dont even touch the ground let alone the wall—Yet the pain of that silver nutcracker with the hand-around handle would have been 'real' I think, and hurry off—Besides of which, whether it's a Locomotive or a Holy Tree they'll bury me under, Emptiness is still the same—

As a chicken enfranchised of its egg, I cut off, in no direction, lyrically, light

A GRAVE LAD FROM LOWELL I revisit the scene of my old school, the second grade at St. Louis presumably—in other words, it's supposed to represent Billings School or St. Louis—in other words, it's not supposed to represent anything but itself—and so sad—First I'm in the cellar which is supposed to be the vast and dark St. Louis Parochial cellar where I remember nuns combing our hair with water from the pisspipes (the little wall falls) and the darkness, dampness, stone, so that nowadays my dreams of the Lowell Hi School basement which was not anywhere as dungeon-like are characterized by the damp gloom of the St. Louis remembered basement—I say remembered because in visiting St. Louis recently it never occurred to me to drop inside and re-see the basement which now in fact as I think about it cannot be located in my real discriminating consciousness—Where was it? the basement of that relatively little redbrick building?—the basement of the Parochial Bazaar hall?—but there's no basement under it!—Where is it but in my mind?—But it is under the redbrick building and so much smaller than I dream and smaller even than the basement of the old High School Freshman Building where the vocational classes were held (wood benches, lathes, the wild Joes ready to begin a new day at their work which always seemed forced on them because they had been caught doing something bad and grownup in the misty gray Lowell)—I revisit this composited basement but suddenly it develops into a real cave, with dirt, dripping unseen walls, vast, but under the school and the further I walk the more it begins to resemble those big caves underneath Market Street in Firsco that I've been dreaming, where recently I found two starving Oriental Japanese soldiers who were grubbing in separate cave rooms—how vast and like the cave underneath Laurier Field where the Big Heart of the Beast was thumping—then I come up to the hallway of the school, the wood planks, the doors to various classes, that sleepy schoolday sun pouring in and it seems I'm revisiting a heretofore completely forgotten "second grade room" which now glimmeringly I recall and cant believe it—the utter lostforever sadness of my unhappiness in one of the front desks of this room, the woman teacher long dead—It's like the Billings School hallways in the background of the little picture of me at age 5, the same mothswarm Buddha-land goldennesses in the dust & and the shadows & the sun & the spectral quiet of Photograph.

AT A CALIFORNIA CAMP the Americans, on orders from the Russians who keep flying overhead in big planes threatening to drop the H-Bomb, have imprisoned a large group of of people in a wire-enclosed trap and are preparing them to be the first victims of the H-Bomb Detonation right on the button. Meanwhile the doomed boys play basketball and even have gang fights. At H-Hour the people will be made to lie down in bomb shelters right under the bomb; some will be given certain shots, some not; offensive liquid mixtures to drink so the cause of your death can be traced like chalk through your guts—Everybody's saying "We'll all die of Mastoids anyway"—"from the concussion on the ears of the upper explosion"—My mother and I are there, trapped, so is Julien, Joe, many others—Ma and I foolishly came to California just in time to be trapped—At H-Hour fools with earphones will hysterically count off the seconds while people wait for death—it is sad—At the end, near the end, Julien and I are sitting together on a step—We have received no shots, we are among the lot who are going to be allowed to die straight without shots and for straight research of our blue remains—It seems to me now that I have been taking care of Julien, who is like a helpless little brother, in many a life, many a rebirth—I am the Bodhisattva entrusted with his care—He barely begins to realize this, I can see, by his new silence and introspective respect—I am writing a poem to commemorate the Scene—it ends with these lines:-

The Silent Hush
Of the Pure Land Thrush.
———meaning Avalokitesvara's Transcendental Sound of Nirvana which is within and beyond the Bomb. It is a great Idealistic Poem and I finish it with a flourish of the pencil, beside the silent non committal Julien whose thoughts are bent on death—It is gray dusk, warm, withered flowers lay around—

The Ground Divine
Of Mortal Mind

I think on waking up—

I'M GOING DOWN THE STONE STEPS of the great Buddhist World Cave saying to watchers on the parapet "It's inward suicide"—and going down the Holy Hall ways with followers, to the big Reclining Face & the swarming dark full of light irradiating from the Center—there's nowhere to go but inward—The Cave of the World, the Cave of Reality beyond conceptions of sun, air, etc., contains the Well of Shining Reality

I'M RUNNING DOWN a sidehill & a goat-bull or cow-goat hackled to a long chain starts chasing me, I figure "All I gotta do is run so far & she'll reach the end of her rope" but instead of sprinting I keep twisting around to put my hand on the cow's head like Manolete appeasing & jibing the bull, but now this particular dream-cow takes bite painful bites at my hand & I twist to always afraid I will be butted up in the air, so foolishly I keep turning again (like halfback in flight catching bullet passes just behind over center & twists while running on delicate ankles that interlace as he goes one circle around with the ball hauled in)—but this is no hero football game, that cow is taking Pink Chagall bites out of me & it's a night mare I dont even wake from with an issue decided—Besides what's the issue? Empty cows.

PREVIOUS, EISENHOWER is president of heroic America thru gray decades up to 1980's and we're all amazed to see him champion childlike cause after childlike cause, arms folded, a Saint, & I like him.—Cant afford to hate him 'cause I'm a child—Passing new paper laws, deep dream laws applied to childlike civilizations on an arbitrary gray map called the world—I cant remember the details of this bottomlessly gone dream, on waking I had no recollection or wanted more even of the barest details concerning what the Lincoln-like heroic laws were that E. passed but it seems I knew him in a dark house where's a Tolstoyan dance going on & events & crash!—nobody loves me 'cause there's no me.

I'M SITTING IN THE WINDOW of our new kitchen in Brooklyn & as I gaze happily at all the golden windows of the tenements in the soft & fragrant dark outside, like the dark of California, my Mother is telling me not to sit in the window with the light on or the Snipers'll get me, a new secret juvenile organization dedicated to shooting people in windows—but I dont believe in the existence of the Snipers so I sit there, glad to be home anyway—And later I'm walking down Brooklyn Cow Street with Hindenburg & Huck the hoodlums of Times Square who've become involved with me again & come to get me at my cellardoor—This white dream we're having is truly inwardly and actually as peaceful, and ultimately, as the meditations of a devout priest in his church at 4 o'clock in the afternoon——as he gazes at his breviary, or through it,

I FIND CODY IN THE RAMPBACK at the race track, he solemnly shows me his new theory of how to beat the horses, it's an English newspaper clipping and the whole thing is worked out—Earlier Garden also had a theory, about snakes, insects, worms, and for proof he takes a hairy caterpillar and eats it as I <u>ack</u> and then like a child I can see his whitemush openmouth as he chews semi-seriously, it's on the high tenement of Mrs. LaMartine's porch in Centreville Lowell

Theories shmeories!
..new ways of losing and uglying

MAYBE THE REASON WHY PEOPLE DONT WRITE TO ME ANY MORE is because I'm such an out and out bum—Tonight, or rather this gray morning, I dream'd I was in and out of apartment houses presumably in N.Y. on shady maneuvers (to get a place to sleep) with Deni Bleu and other tramps also trying to get coats—at one point I'm riding along on a sky elevator and I see what I remember to be James Watson's pad but the kitchen with its new brown furniture is different (far shot from dark sad brown wood of Lowell Kitchens long ago dusks)—because of furniture I think "Oh it's not his place!" but on calling and investigating it is, but James wont receive me, he's been in there 2 years with his girl "holed up" loving and writhing and writing—I sneak around doormen into foyers of the city, I'm wearing a suspicious overcoat, no hat, no morals, no scruples—not a thief but a strange gelatinous nameless mooch, a hanger onner, a parasite, a city wart, an apartment haunter, a sneaker-in-halls, a mattress-bug, a voyeur of orgies, a disgusting stale spectre—a dream drifter—at one point I'm hitch hiking up at that endless hopeless hill highway the other side of Bonny Brae—no rides, I sneak in subsidiary fields—Finally with a round quarter I find my way to a lunchcart near the r.r. station which has drastically reduced its prices in half, and would have gone in anyway from weariness and so with all the other customers,—Ice cream a dish is only a dime, I order it from the new queer counterman assistant who is a big good looking frank fairy who gives me the ice cream but forgets to hand me my 15¢ change because a boy at a booth has presumed to pull his leg (manfully) by saying "I'll suck your big juicy cock anytime" and Our Hero jumps without shame over the counter & goes to sit seriously in the booth to discuss further, as all the men notice and smile—So I figure I'll wait and get my change and meanwhile buy a 15¢ dish of hot pudding which will be free at the pay-counter when I remind Lover Man—as I'm taking my tray and silver with women in come two railroad guards one of them 300 pounds, and they pull up antiquated sorta car-seats to the counter and sit low to the floor facing it, waiting to be served, wearing old button down sweaters and guard badges and smoking pipes in the ray of the afternoon sun pouring into the busy lunchroom—

THAT RECURRENT DREAM WHERE I'M ALWAYS IN CALIFORNIA in Frisco, and have to travel all the way back and have no money—I see a woman suspended in mid-air giving her son a strange rich pie thru a window of a wooden Frisco building, which he accepts graciously over the rushing traffics of the street, and I think first of Evelyn (Pomeray) in Los Gatos and the sad trains there-to, then I think of Ma in the East (N. Y. ?) and how I gotta go home for Christmas—There've been events all night, a bloody season, Irwin Gardens everywhere, Codies, et ceteras, I've had my up-to-here—it's time to go—wearing that seedy old topcoat and my muffcap over my ears there I go driving down the spectral boulevard in an old car (it's actually Cody's '40 Packard) and I think of hitch hiking all in the snow and decide, "Wyoming? No! I'll just drive all the way, at same time get this car home" (it's been given me)—What will I do for gas money? from hitch hikers—I'll work! "But if I work I wont make it for Christmas!"—the whole spectral hump o the continent's ahead a me, ephemeral as snow, awful as Edom,—my Arcady of Ribs, my Troy of Bones I'll crack and Waterloo on such a hopeless run and as if not remarmant & cartchaptoed enuf and once again and <u>again again!</u>—but here I am already, driving wrong way on the Oneway boulevard and seeing I cant turnoff I make a neat proud U-turn and go back where I started from still debatin how to make that 3,000 miles east, in that miserable coat and muff hat, driving slow like an old man, sunk low at the seat—"La Marde"—and all on account of a pie.

What an arbitrary conception this Coming Home For Christmas is—I've done it twice now, and each time it bugged out on me—the first time my mother fell asleep, the second time she had to go to a funeral—big gay cities have huge sad cemeteries right outside, need em—

Rattling tenements and spectral girls (I

call em tenements, I mean the wooden houses of San Fran)—(like the one Rosemarie jumped off-of)—this drear dreaming of necessitous sad traveling and I wake up in a vast comfortable double bed in Rocky Mount in a house in the country with nothing to do but write Visions of Gerard, wash the dishes and feed the cat!—and pop the Book of Dreams—Cant remember the haunting taunting earlier details of this dream, the girls, cops, floors, sex, suicides, pies, pastiches, parturiences, wallpapers, transcendencies—the stations, gray—Garden, who never laughs, mines information—June Ogilvie Blabbery Adams McCracken my girl—June John Boabus Protapolapalopos the the Greek All-Mix Lover—Pain Twang—

PRIVATE SCHINE, the blond sad handsome boy who was on TV in the Army-McCarthy hearings, is, now, years later, still held in an Army prison-madhouse where they've been trying to establish his "insanity" all these years—for anti-McCarthy political reasons—You see him in green fatigues, standing with his interlocutor, before a TV camera, as they bring up patients, the first one vaguely in my dream I think a gibbering idiot, and Schine is asked: "Is he insane?"

"Insane"

Schine is weary, you can tell this has been going on so long it's like routine but horror.

They bring up an ordinary looking young lad in fatigue & cap.

"Is he a queer?"

"Queer"—wearily, and I do a doubletake seeing the kid.

Then they bring up two fellows together: says the interlocutor: "<u>Two immortals who have become mortal.</u> Insane??"

And Schine bursts into tears—

And it's that old railyard scene, nearby, near the waterfront, cold, the bakeries and warehouses, this hopeless world—

I rush to Joe McCarthy to tell him but he's helpless and hopeless too—in the marble halls of Congress

I'M WALKING WITH EDNA in the mud roads beyond Mexico City downtown, in the slums, we're looking ahead at the hopeless horizon we're trying to reach on foot, I dont know how many hundreds of miles it is, all I know is we better take a train or bus to get there, a bright El Dorado up ahead in the eerie rainy Mexico o' my dreams—But finally I tell Edna let's do it now, here, she keeps looking over her shoulder down the empty night street, we find and occupy a latrine and starts she wants to lower her skirt I say no just lift it, and we start, cant get in, but I lift her thigh with one hand and now it's so perfect she herself has forgotten where she is and I wake up rocking the whole bed —lost the wife of my youth, so I deserved these nocturnal tortures—Edna was young in the dream, too

At another point, back at that strange marble-building-hotel point of MexCity, I'm smirkin with myself that I'm gonna get a girl in the streets beyond where the first (1950) MexCity dreams were, where Dave Sherman had lost his pants—I'll have to find a new and special language now to begin describing the indescribale location-mystery of these dream-locations for they're important —in each of these locations lurks a mystery of _Character_, a _Vision_—

G.J.'S. MOTHER AND SISTER are cooking awful messes in a black and gloomy kitchen in Greek Mexico City that I eat, it's like a blue jello inside a rind of hog-glue-skin, and's made by putting the jello uncolored in a cloth bag with the blue dye and some sawdusty stuff and letting it stand (in the grime, presumably)—G.J. is so solemn and serious and hungry I fain would eat with him, and do—O where is the Lost G.J. of a Black Greek Mexico City dream?—he's a kid again, and has that crazy potentiality, potency, of language, of making me laugh, amazing me —outside are all those endless riots of streets and marquees of downtown and black gloom roads and alleys—

A Mexico City fit for Fellaheen Angels—St. Gloom,—St. Wild & Crazy—Some Tibetan remembrance, some ghee and tallow-kitchen for G.J.-SOUL and I when we were young in Darkland and I joyed to see the Light of his Gloomy Prophecies—as we go foraging in the rain for garbages and gangs—An epic—Connected with the raggedy LaNegra, too, who must have been our then-time Silvanus Santos and Bodhisattva Hero reminder—

MY DREAM NIGHTJOB for the past several years of dreaming, I'm going to it at night in a fabulous 4-story-high bus across the railroad tracks near that perennial Brooklyn like Pittsburgh like waterfront, around midnight, and as we bounce over the track I'm reminiscing about my railroad work right on that very track when they'd kicked a boxcar and I threw the switch after it, after it crossed over the points, and then I ran after it and clambered up and braked it to a stop before the deadblock —Proudly, and now as my bus arrives at my nightjob destination "near Yankee Stadium" I gulp and start the great horror of coming down the fourstory busladder on the outside, my hands closing around the grab ladder into tight white fists as I look down at the lucky people on the rain glistening cobbles below—But I negotiate the last 20 feet by half swinging half flying down the ladder and landing in a graceful airy jump to impress workmen, who dont watch—In topcoat and good clothes I clack off to my midnight job (my mindnight job) which is at the office of a garage again, where I know my work so well I'm always deigning to be a little late—Enroute I pass a candy store where just as I'm to buy an ice cold grape soda from the drinkbox some other character occupies the tiny drink-spot before it and I curse—Suddenly I'm some sort of elder brother greedily eating his chocolate pudding and wont give any to the baby, who then, in a William Blake newly-discover'd poem, makes his beautiful complaint

"Is nature
proud?"

and

"Something not new, something not perfumed, something not new, something not perfumed" as he runs his cherubic fingers and counts the panes and missing-panes of the window by his crib with the dusty glass—It is a definite new poem by Blake so beautiful that at points the language of the verse fairly gurgles with babylikeness, just perfect—I can remember long innocent questions complaining about the elder brother's delectable avarice and then the wild witty takeoffs—Ah me—

SOMEDAY I'LL BE REBORN in that great city in another world system, in the past or future, where the single 3-mile high mountain stands against the blue sky—With all my compassion with me, all I'll need is the wisdom of the land

THE BRUNETTE OF MY LIFE—we're approaching a work factory that's shining in the night in a field, (Green School field Centreville), to look for work, when suddenly we start start balling right in the grass—She's Josephine-Maggie Zimmerman like, and throws long sea surges perfectly of her loins back at me—Saying, "I'm going to sleep out here" and I'll go in alone and get a job for us after I come and she'll sleep sweetly in the field like a hobo and wait for me to wake her at dawn—My angel doll of long ago, whose blackhaired presence in my sunny afternoon bedroom I took for granted

I'M IN LOWELL IN A CAFETERIA outside waitingroom on the corner on Kearney Square where the grocery now (I b'lieve) is,—in there is Dick Nietzsche—Shelley Lisle the hepcat of Lowell, at first a lil unfriendly then warming up as I ask him for some bennies and to arrange to buy me more, he dumps about 10 in my hand "Oh they're the new kind!" I cry seeing their perforated bottoms—He lives somewhere in the Dark Highlands like a dark Timmy Clancy of old Lowell dreams, later we'll go there and pick up—I swallow 2 with water at the little icewater fountain and my face lowered to drink pious eyelids fall on swarming death but beyond death Awakening Buddha Realization that earlier I'd been up the (Concord) River of Eternity (the true Mississippi), the sere shores, and I recall my Ma would be mad to see me get high and dissipate but "It's the pure truth no matter what you do" I realize piously drinking and outside it's gray Kearney Sq. so sad and same and strange with dead ghosts waiting for buses, and damp foyers of marble halls, and rain and bus stops and wetshoes—I dig Dick as a great new sad kid—

THE MERCHANT MARINE ACADEMY is drumming out two impostors who pretended to be officers on the ship, as a remnant of oldtime punishments the ritual now is to lead them out with a black velvet doublenoose around both their necks and march off the merchantship between erect files of cadets, to drums—I see the captain who is reading the sentence: "The squawk of the little very self which wanders everywhere..........."

"THE IMMATERIAL MEADOW OF THIS WORLD you ask as with golden ash" is saying the pockmarked colored kid with glasses wearing a snow white sweater to which I am clutching unconscious of what I'm doing as he's turned in his schooldesk seat talking to the blond kid disciple next to me who wanted to know and I'm thinking "All this arbitrary interest of mine in teachings, 't' ends up I put my face close to ugly pockmarks and badbreath" and stop clutching at his sweater—Earlier the Master had just read from the Sutra:- "It is not so with the wise, the elite, they see unconditioned void perfection of freedom, but those who discriminate appearances are the 'niggers'"—(in the sense that he would have meant the 'niggers' the ignorant and simpleminded)—nevertheless this pockmarked kid is the smartest—Where have I seen a pockmarked bespectacled black man dressed in snow? Gandhi? Jimmy Thomas? Some Jain in olden

incarnations i the wood?
i the immaterial
meadow of this world?

DRIVING WITH MY DETECTIVE PUBLISHER FRIEND down a dry sand road that runs parallel to Bayshore Hi-way but by itself in dry desert Pecos rocks and blasted arroyos of red and orange dust, we come to his isolate cottage, Joe Louis is there but leaves during dinner to go home to his kids—another crazy Negro is in the garage

I HAD A WHITE BANDAGE on my head from a wound, the police are after me around the dark stairs of wood near the Victory Theater in Lowell, I sneak away—come to the boulevard where a parade of children chanting my name hide me from the searching police as I duck along their endless ranks, keeping low—The parade of children is endless—Chanting and singing we go marching into Mon-

golia with me with my white bandaged head in front
(dreamed the day after the publication of ON THE ROAD)

AS CAPTAIN OF THE GREAT VAGUE BOAT I've neglected my duties playing around with passengers up & down a thousand spectral staircases, suddenly I realize we've been at sea three days with nobody steering, I go to the dark bridge house, try to turn on the lights, and suddenly a big Chinese Strange Freighter going the other way signals me, I reply with one pull on the whistle rope, VOOOM, then fearing that "one-long" will be taken for distress & my peaceful vague sea voyage captaincy disturbed by boarding officials and breeches' buoys & signing of papers I hold off I give another short pull, this time because of my hysteria the whistle just goes PLURP—So I steer, cant see, hope we dont ram ships—Arriving at a tiny port with a narrow canal I veer the immense front of the ship around curves hoping all that hugeness behind me isnt ruining villages—

NIGHTMARE IN NORTHPORT—last night, the three who started of as Bull and Irwin and me naked, later steal in China and escape on the run in a big Movie Award Running Classic about running up over the mad continental mountain and down into the back of India, safe, except for border guards and the shopkeeping informer whom they jump and start murdering with knives and kicking in the face WHAP! & finally face to face glued with blood the hero pukes up yellow sticky glue puke that glues their faces together in puky blood so that when he looks up in disgust great messes like on top of pizza pie stretch and the brothers recoil and exclaim "He's Sioux Sick!" and I wake up in the quiet 4 AM and ask quietly "Jesus, pourquoi tu'm montre des portraits comme ça?' and meditate crosslegged realizing it must be an educational movie from another Buddhaland showing Bodhisattvas why to reject violence and how horrible ignorance which not only projects an outside world but grasps at it, fights in it—It was the only really horrible nightmare I ever had, got it from a beebite earlier in the day I think.

The actual description of that horrified yellow puking of China mixed with the bloody faces would make you sick

DIGGING GRAVES IN THE YARD, I've already dug my father's along the walk and the marks are still there but now (and also dug a woman's but didnt place her in) but I'm afraid I wont dig deep enough under the 3 feet of snow and now have to dig 2 for Jerry & Lola and say to two guys with me "Come Spring the snow melts you see elbows sticking out of the ground, gad what a thing to be buried in a black suit" and one of the guys is suddenly tall looking at me in a black suit!

—Cold bony dream—

HORRIBLE, I GUESS IT'S THE END OF THE WORLD, the clouds in the sky are soot black and turn to white as you look and suddenly they are dancing a little on a tilty horizon so, and like on a ship's deck I realize it's not the clouds moving it's the Earth & I tell it to the gang in the school yard "The earth is moving" and Irwin and I go back and stand together near the redbrick schoolwall to marvel that the Apocalypse has finally come and we're together in its Moment--Meanwhile my mother'd followed people up the steep hill and tried to sit crawling out over the mile high seats and I had to help her—

MY ASS NAKED sitting on a stool in the field full of people I'm reading some book and the Jack Paar show is going on in the field but I dont care—Suddenly he comes up with mike and camera and pins me down to have me televised universally naked, I hang there like a helpless child till I hear Julien's faint voice in back trees saying (twangily St. Louis) "Dont let him do it!" so after a helpless moment I up and throw him a feeble punch

THE 500 MILE HIGH WINDOWS of the Tangiers yellow light night—Starts with a Nazi officer leading me up a snowy hill to execute me via automatic shnortzel Luger and makes German jokes in the falling snow making me think "O why do these dreary sexual executioners always have to come on so dull with their tired-out straight jokes" and when we come to a house with a steep outdoor stairway he orders me to climb, which I do (it is the same stairway of the cops in Lowell when I had the white bandage that I escaped to Mongolia in, as children paraded in my name), I know he's going to shoot me in the back so I climb and wince to feel it but nothing happens and when I get to the top I turn and see he's having difficulty with his Luger—in the snow—by the same mountain pass that those Chinese-Indians used to go down the India border in the yellow puke dream—So I escape into a V-cornered tenement room and look out the window and in the dream it says it's a 500 mile drop to the street (tho you can see from yellow Tangiers nightlights below it's really 500 stories or so)—It turns into a movie which me and my gang are going up a long night boulevard of transcontinental bus travelers to see, after I buy my thin little ice cream cone I'm walking with my friends one of whom is in drag as the Thief of Baghdad hero of the story (worn out Gene Kelly), another is real out queer Genêt hero, and there's Irwin, Simon, others—In my dream I realize 'butch drag' for the first time clearly and sympathize—I'm kinda weird myself, as I yell something at a group of girls and they come on dikey with me on the boulevard—Gang goes into the immense 500 mile high balcony and it shows the hero at the window ledge of the top floor, then a boom descends thru the 500 mile high tenement to show the audience the enormity of the dancing halls and props all the way down to the street where fallers squash on newspaper sidewalk and we're sitting together in a box and Irwin in a cultured concerned complaint classically angelic says "Oh, _let_ them have a big ball!" meaning all these Tangerian 500 mile queer teaheads their halls and dancing balls in this weird Arabian nightlife town (sea nearby) and it's so funny I giggle wonderfully like Cody and the whole gang turns and guffaws to realize I'm still at their rear, guarding and digging—Meanwhile groups are leaving the theater and see us (such a strange group) and others nearby also strange, all boys, all intelligent looking, and say "Oh ho, you can tell it's Saturday night"

—In the dream I'm a cultured queer queen-king, part saint, beloved—On waking it seemed I remembered that girl on the boulevard in my previous lifetime in England whom I must have murdered—I must have been a queer in that previous lifetime or couldnt divine about "butch drag" without experience in this lifetime—

TO GET DOWN FROM OUR APARTMENT to the street you have to go down a ladder overhanging from the top of the Empire State Building—I'm sick of the whole fucking thing and refuse to do it again but Jesse does it—A man had just tried it before her (going to work with evening paper in his pocket) and he queitly dropped off and fell to death silently and unobtrusively—It happens all the time—But I go down the safe way which is not indicated in the dream and I'm down on the dark street strolling wondering if Jesse made it—Turn around and see her a block up strolling slowly on the other side of the street—It seems Ma didnt make it and is dead but I dont believe it—(The same day Ma was scared coming down the attic ladder, dreams prevision in a strange tender way)—Jesse is strolling sadly in the dark not knowing where I am any more

A FANCY DRESSED WOMAN is remorsefully sneaking out on her wailing baby to step out with tophatted Shadows in the city night, she leaves, sneaks downstairs and just then a woman upstairs comes down tip toeing in stockinged feet to watch the neglectful lady sneak out—but I am sitting in the dark watching it all thru a hall window, I see the peeking woman's satisfied smile and know that in a moment she will horrifiedly notice that she was watched in the act of her Spy—and when she does see me it's just a dim light on my face in the dark and what a leering smile I give her! she blanches

CROSSING MOODY STREET BRIDGE with a holy goat in my arms I let him down on the planks and he runs across the street and vaults the rail of the bridge clean down to death on the water-crashing rocks below—I cant look—But suddenly I realize he's swimming beneath the bridge, apparently missed the rocks, and now I see him swimming strongly to the rocky shore—He makes it, comes in the underbridge ramp running to me and as I reach down fingertips to catch him in my arms he stands on hind legs and just hooves my fingertips—I know I'll get him by the feet, haul him up, and take him home—

that Lamb
(white)

I'M IN MEXICO PEERING INTO WINDOWS while neighbors stare, finally I ask one woman "A donde es Senor Gaines?" but I really mean Hubbard and shows me a window with Hubbard inside standing in the middle of his room surrounded by a dozen beatnik and hoodlum and other visitors—I knock on window, he rushes out politely to let me in but I have my hunting cap over my eyes not even looking at him and go in—In the middle of the floor Bull (no room for himself to sit) expounds on guns and finally fishes out a small automatic from a silk wrapping & hands it to a young darkhaired hoodlum—Later, in his shorts like the John L. Sullivan boxing-pose photo in BIG TABLE magazine, Bull is advised by the Sergeant to report up the sandbank to his officers the "Allies"—Other guys in shorts are listening—I marvel that Bull is so sardonic with the sergeant & about the whole Army in general—"Give my regards to the Allies," says I, "if you gets there" (imitating Charles Laughton for Bull's benefit & also knowing he wont even go) & Bull laughs but I lamely add "<u>When</u> you gets there," as always nervous when trying to be funny for Bull, & like in the door with the hunting cap he politely refrains from comments on my awkwardness—I marvel at the respect he gets from the men and officers of the world

A BIG 'BEAT GENERATION CONVENTION' is arranged in Philadelphia, everybody's there but they've erected a 300 foot tower of concrete which topples over & falls in the field, you see nimble workmen sneaking out of the wood board interior amazingly & some being run over as the tower is allowed to roll because they're letting the rabbits inside move it shifting their positions—I see Irwin & Simon but I'm not sitting with them—On the way back to New York I'm with one of the Conference officials and when I ask him what he got out of the conference he says "O I'm not interested in that, I just provided the concrete for the tower" and I realize he's just a gangster and he gets real mean and shows me how Frank Sinatra wallops guys on the jaw (holding my head and almost blasting me with his big fist) —I hate him—You next see F.B.I. men studying his accounts showing where a certain "Gleason" received $6,000 in the phoney concrete deal—"We're interested in knowing who this Gleason really is"—They've trapped the gangster inside his house—In between I'd come down that amazing ski-run shaft street steeper than belief, the same as in Lowell sometimes, James Watson nods when I tell him I wish we had sleds, we're coming down via the endless elevated steps of upper Bronx New York—I get sick & almost die as I fly around a post (wake up with a neuralgic leg)—

Everybody at the conference had been sitting in pairs, in chairs, I forget the fellow I sat with but in the back of the hall Jerry Getty has been balling the beautiful Revlon Announcer Girl Starlet & I want some too, I find them comin out from a dark sewer secret door & she's naked & Jerry says "She's out of her mind"—I grab her warm naked body, she doesnt want me—I dont like her much

THE FLYING HORSES OF MIEN MO—I'm riding a bus thru Mexico with Cody sleeping at my side, at the dawn the bus stops in the countryside and I look out at the quiet warm fields & think: "Is this really Mexico? why am I here?" —The fields look too calm & grassy & bugless to be Mexico —Later I'm sitting on the other side of the bus, Cody is gone, I look up in the sky & see that old ten thousand foot or hundred mile high mountain cliff with its enormous hazy blue palaces and temples where they have giant granite benches & tables for Giant Gods bigger than the ones who hugged skyscrapers on Wall Street—And in the air, Ah the silence of that horror, I see flying winged horses with capes furling over their shoulders, the slow majestic pawing of their front hooves as they clam thru the air flight—Griffins they are!—So I realize we're in "Coyocan" & this is the famous legendary place—I start telling 4 Mexicans in the seat in front of me the story of the Mountain of

Coyocan & its Secret Horses but they laugh not only to hear a stranger talk about it but the ridiculousness of anybody even mentioning or noticing it—There's some secret they wont tell me concerning ignoration of the Frightful Castle—They even get wise with Gringo Me and I feel sand pouring down my shirt front, the big Mexican is sitting there with sand in his hand, smiling—I leap up & grab one, he is very tiny & skinny & I hold his hand against his belly so he wont pull a knife on me but he has none—They're really laughing at me for my big ideas about the Mountain—

We arrive at Coyocan town over which the hazy blue Mountain rises and now I notice that the Flying Horses are constantly swirling over this town & around the cliff, swooping, flying, sometimes sweeping low, yet nobody looks up & bothers with them—I cant bring myself to believe that they are actually flying horses & I look & look but that's what they have to be, even when I see them in moon profile: horses pawing thru air, slow, slow, eerie griffin horror men-horses—I realize they've been there all the time swirling around the Eternal Mountain Temple & I think: "The bastards have something to do with that Temple, that's where they come from, I always knew that Mountain was all horror!"—I go inside the Coyocan Maritime Union Hall to sign for a Chinese sea job, it's in the middle of Mexico, I dont know why I've come all the way from New York to the landlocked center of Mexico for a sea voyage but there it is: a Seaman's hiring hall full of confusion & pale officials who dont understand why I came also—One of them makes a great intelligent effort to have letters in duplicate written to New York to begin straightening out the reason why I came—So if it's a job I'll get, it wont be for a week at least, or <u>more</u>—The town is evil & completely sinister because everybody is ugly sneering (the natives, I mean,) and they refuse to recognize the existence of that Terrible Swirl of Flying horses—"Mien Mo," I think, remembering the name of the Mountain in Burma they call the world, with Dzapoudiba the southern island (India), on account of Himalayan secret horrors—The beating heart of the Giant Beast is up there, the Griffins are just incidental insects—but those Flying Horses are happy! how beautifully they claw slow fore-hooves thru the blue void!—

Meanwhile 2 young American seamen and I study them flying up there miles high & watch them swoop lower, when they come low they change into blue and white birds to fool everybody—Even I say: "Yep, they're not flying horses, they only seem to be, they're Birds!" but even as I say that I see a distinct horse motioning lyrically thru the moon with a cape furling from his infernal shoulders—

A broken nosed ex boxer approaches me hinting that for 50¢ a job can be arranged on a ship—He is so sinister & intense I'm afraid to even give him 50¢ —Up comes a blonde with her fiance announcing her forthcoming marriage but she interrupts her speech every now and then to wail on my joint in front of everybody in the streets of COYOCAN!

And the Flying Horses of Mien Mo are galloping with silent ease in the happy empty air way up there—Tinkle Tinkle go the streets of Coyocan as the sun falls, but up there is all silence & the Giant Gods are up— How can I describe it?

STRANGE STRANGE DREAM of me making myself into a previous masturbating tape recorded body which lies right beside me whacking my hammer...

DREAMED I WAS WAITING in a strange illuminated white bus terminal in New Jersey for the bus to New York, endless wait, and there's a beautiful but strange Chinese woman waiting against the wall—I go up to her & point out the two Chinese boys & two Negro boys also waiting—"How's that for a picture?" I banter, and come to feel her girdle, which she doesnt like—"How old are you?" I ask staring at the strange serene oval beauty of her face & she says "Let us just let it go at that, I was born in 1863" and I understand counting immediately that she's almost one hundred years old & I say "I see, you're Tibetan" and she gives a slight nod with her eyes—The bus is coming at four and it's only three in dismal Sunday New Jersey

WE ALL STAND FOR A GROUP PHOTOGRAPH in the yard of the great Pine Tree Mansion of the Captors—later we play in the field, a hundred of us, I see Cody giving the rear man's hiball sign to a departing freight train & places a little Brakeman Doll in the tracks who also cranked-up tinily gives same sign as the train goes off to the outer world—We're all prisoners of the Communists—Finally they ask us back for that group photo on the lawn leeringly saying "Quite a few faces missing!" which I notice is true as I'm the last one to appear & the ranked standers are depleted—But they wave me away from the picture contemptuously down the dungeon steps, I've been suspected of revolutionary or at least bugged tendencies as I yakked in the "Free Field"—Down I go to my doom—An insane attendant down the brown stone steps has me sit temporarily in a cell which has a large pool of brown water in a big pan with shit floating in it while I'm to be processed by him but he leaves momentarily on a call so I rock the cell shiplike somehow & dump the brown shit water out into the dungeon aisle—But he gets back just as I'm doing it, picks up the "pan" and dumps it on my head and then on _his_ head and we stare at each other dripping brown shit-water hair & I realize among other things that the attendants of the Lower Hells are so miserably agonized they want you to be the same as they—But meanwhile I understand that the Underground Prisons have women cooks & waitresses who need man-love so badly that they have developed a super secret subterranean system of their own to hie men away into sumptuous underground lovemaking apartments & the Authorities never know where they've vanished—The secret word is so secret & feminine, the tokens of admission to stud so mysterious, you can spend the rest of your captive life just boffing these luscious thin blondes completely secure & safe from harm—The "tokens" are supposed to be "food ration" buttons but they're really what the women gather in work and pay to be allowed to visit the hidden captive men-places to be laid—And the Captor Authorities are forever puzzled—The insane attendant with shit water in his hair doesnt even know what's happened to you after you've been spirited away from his jurisdiction, not to mention the outside Firingsquad Photographers of the "Free Yard"